'I won't stay h

'You want a long ... that's what you wa... too much time and ... now, so don't try to fight me, Isabelle, because I *will* have you, and on my terms!' Jean-Luc's hand tightened on her wrist. 'Now get in the car! You're coming home with me!'

Dear Reader

Welcome to Monaco, the tiny principality on the coast of southern France that glitters with majestic wealth and jet-set glamour. A fairy-tale come true, its past and its present are littered with romance — what better location for our latest Euromance?

The Editor

The author says:

'I can't remember a time when I didn't love the name "Monaco", but I was seventeen when I first drove down the Moyenne Corniche and into Monte-Carlo. Since then, I've been back many times. At nineteen, with a gorgeous French boyfriend, in a white open-topped sports car. At twenty-two, when I lived in Antibes, and attended the Monte-Carlo Grand Prix. At twenty-five, with a bunch of British pop musicians; and at twenty-eight, on my way to a concert in Italy, stopping in Monte-Carlo for coffee at midnight. I always read everything I see about Monaco, but most particularly about Princess Caroline, who is three years my senior, and one of the women I admire most in the world.'

Sarah Holland

★ TURN TO THE BACK PAGES OF THIS BOOK FOR *WELCOME TO EUROPE*. . .OUR FASCINATING FACT-FILE ★

DANGEROUS DESIRE

BY

SARAH HOLLAND

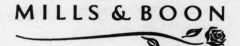

MILLS & BOON

MILLS & BOON LIMITED
ETON HOUSE, 18–24 PARADISE ROAD
RICHMOND, SURREY, TW9 1SR

MILLS & BOON and the Rose Device
are trademarks of the publisher.

First published in Great Britain 1994
by Mills & Boon Limited

© Sarah Holland 1994

Australian copyright 1994   Philippine copyright 1994
This edition 1994

ISBN 0 263 78544 0

Set in 10 on 11½ pt Linotron Times
01-9407-53129

Typeset in Great Britain by Centracet, Cambridge
Made and printed in Great Britain

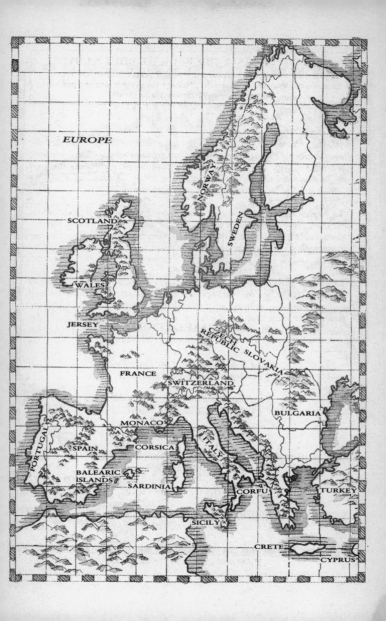

CHAPTER ONE

THEY came through Customs at Nice airport, trolleys laden with suitcases, and the jackets they had worn when they'd left Paris. People bustled everywhere across the gleaming airport lounge.

Isabelle walked with a Southern belle sway, her long red hair gleaming down her slender, sexy back, the curves of her body and the flash of her green eyes attracting double-takes from admiring Frenchmen.

'The taxi drive to Monaco is only forty-five minutes,' Marie-Claire told her. 'We'll be home by one o'clock central European time.'

'I can't wait!' Isabelle said, her French fluent, but softened slightly with that Louisiana accent still clinging to her vowels. 'I've wanted to go to Monaco all my life!'

The glass doors slid open elctronically. Heat assailed them from all sides. A row of Citroën taxis gleamed in the hot sunlight, palm trees waving softly in the ninety-eight-degree breeze.

'Mmm! It's hot and southern, just like home!' Isabelle drawled as the warm air clung to her peachy skin.

'I thought France was your home now!' Marie-Claire laughed, looking around for a taxi.

'Well, it is for the moment,' she agreed, because something told her she would never go back to New Orleans, not after what had happened, not now that she was beginning to feel pretty again for the first time.

Suddenly, a long white chauffeur-driven Rolls-

Royce Corniche drew up. The roof was down. A man reclined in the back, black hair flickering around a tanned, hard-boned face with dark glasses and a tough mouth as he stared up unseeingly at the palm trees and the blue sky.

'*Oh, mon Dieu!*' Marie-Claire clapped a hand to her cheek. 'It's my brother!'

Isabelle felt every hackle in her rising as she recognised him. Jean-Luc Ferrat, the infamous multi-millionaire who liked fast cars, fast women and life in the fast lane. He was the kind of man she hated with a vengeance, a very justified vengeance, and the arrogant air with which he lay back, studying the sky from the back of his flashy car, made her want to slap his handsome face. She was angrily aware of how irrational her reaction to him was, but feelings were feelings, and she was as helpless against hers as anybody else against theirs. The best one could do was hope one did not express them as irrationally as one felt them.

'What on earth is he doing here?' Marie-Claire was saying. 'He's supposed to be in Nassau for the summer!'

'You mean he's going back to Monaco? To the apartment?' Isabelle was rigid. 'He'll be actually living there with us?'

'I don't know. . .' Marie-Claire knew exactly how Isabelle felt about rich, dynamic playboys. 'I'll go and ask him.'

Jean-Luc Ferrat was getting out of the car, formidably tall, savagely handsome and wearing a fifty-thousand-franc grey Armani suit.

'Marie-Claire! *Ça va*?' He bent his dark head for a kiss, the French way—three, one on each cheek to signify close friends or family.

'Ça va, cheri — but what are you doing here?'

'My business in Nassau was wrapped up quickly.' He glanced away from her, saw Isabelle and did a double-take, then slowly slid his dark glasses off to see her better. 'I came home last night. . .'

Isabelle tensed angrily as he continued speaking to his sister while his jet-black eyes flashed over Isabelle's body with open sexual appraisal in their dark, cynical depths. Her irrational feelings swamped her in a rush of fury. She arched haughty brows at him, her green eyes filled with contempt, and looked him up and down as though he were a street-urchin.

'. . . fired and replaced several people.' He was still staring at Isabelle. 'I'm home for the rest of the summer.'

Marie-Claire sighed. 'How very inconvenient.'

'Why?' he murmured, glancing at his sister.

'Because I'm home for the summer, too! And I brought my flatmate home from Paris with me.'

'Your flatmate? Ah, yes. The sad American girl. You told me about her. Where is she?'

'Over there.' Marie-Claire turned and pointed.

Jean-Luc's dark head whipped round, his face reflecting shock as he stared at Isabelle. There was a brief silence. Then he said thickly, 'She is your American flatmate? Her? The redhead over there in the green dress?'

'Yes, and she's staying for six weeks,' Marie-Claire said, dwarfed by her brother, who must have been about six feet four and in the peak of male physical condition. 'Do you mind?'

'Far from it,' he murmured, and strode like a predatory jungle animal, rippling with muscle beneath that Armani suit, to tower in front of Isabelle, dwarfing her too and making her prickle with his sheer sexual menace as he extended a very strong, tanned hand and said smokily, '*Enchanté, mademoiselle. Je suis Jean-Luc Ferrat, et* ——'

'Yes, I recognised you.' Isabelle withdrew her hand quickly and arched haughty brows. 'When you were staring at me just now, *monsieur*, as though I were a mannequin in a shop window!'

His black lashes flickered. 'Forgive me, *mademoiselle*.' He gave a slow sardonic smile. 'I didn't realise you were my sister's friend.'

She gave a polite nod, and said, 'My name is Isabelle Montranix. I understand I'm to be staying at your apartment. I — I'm very pleased to meet you, as you're Marie-Claire's brother.'

'But not as myself? I'm sorry to hear that, *mademoiselle*. Perhaps during your stay you will allow me to change your mind.'

Her mouth tightened. 'Perhaps!'

'You're staying for the summer?'

'Yes.' Her face was cool and haughty. 'If that's OK.'

'It's more than OK,' he murmured, lifting his eyes to hers. 'My sister didn't tell me her American flatmate was so strikingly beautiful.'

Her heart beat too fast suddenly, because he looked at her intimately, as though he already knew he would kiss her, slide her clothes off with his expert hands, and make very practised love to her. It was a look she had no doubt he had practised a million times before on other women. She detested him for it — mainly because it was so effective. There was nothing more despicable than a skilled womaniser, and Jean-Luc Ferrat was nothing if not that.

'So.' Jean-Luc glanced at his sister. 'I'm going home now in the helicopter. Can I give you both a lift?'

'In the chopper?' Marie-Claire clapped her hands. 'Whee!'

He gave her an indulgent smile. '*Bébé*!'

Marie-Claire fluttered her eyelashes at him and he laughed.

'Are these your cases?' He turned, snapped his fingers at the chauffeur who was waiting obediently. 'Take these to the helicopter, then drive the Rolls back to Monaco.'

'*Oui*, Monsieur Ferrat!' The chauffeur leapt to his command.

'Come.' Jean-Luc turned on his heel and strode into the airport building with a threatening masculinity that drew admiring glances from every woman in the vicinity.

Isabelle's skin prickled with hostility as she stared after him.

'We'll be home in twenty minutes now!' laughed Marie-Claire. 'And your first view of Monaco will be the most spectacular!'

They followed Jean-Luc, and Isabelle thought of the first time she had seen him.

His savagely handsome face had been on the cover of *Paris-Match* the month Isabelle had first arrived in France, three years ago, and she could remember every photograph in the magazine layout as if she had read it only yesterday. . . Jean-Luc in his Ferrari, Jean-Luc in his private jet, Jean-Luc seducing a woman in a sunlit field, unaware of the paparazzi's close-up lens trained on him.

Just like Anthony! She had thought with hatred and contempt for the man who had ruined her life, and that was what she thought now as she walked behind Jean-Luc Ferrat — that he was just like Anthony. A

conceited swine, a womaniser, a liar, a cheat and
thoroughly dangerous.

When she'd met and become friendly with Marie-
Claire, she had had no idea that the infamous Jean-
Luc Ferrat was her elder brother. Marie-Claire hated
the paparazzi and also hated social climbers. She was
very cautious about letting people know who she was,
and it had not been until she'd invited Isabelle to
Monaco for the summer, and Isabelle had accepted,
that she had finally confessed to her true background.

'Do you mind very much that Jean-Luc will be here
with us?' Marie-Claire asked her now. 'I really did
think he'd be away all summer.'

'Of course not,' Isabelle said with a false smile.

'You do mind, though, and I don't blame you.'
Marie-Claire sighed. 'I know how you feel about —
well, you know. About Anthony. And I'm so sorry
this has happened. But Jean-Luc really isn't as bad
as — '

'It's not your fault.' She patted her hand. 'I'll just
keep out of his way. After all, I'm probably not his
type.'

'Not his type?' Marie-Claire frowned. 'Are you
crazy? You've practically got his initials stamped on
your forehead! I saw the way he was staring at you,
Isabelle, and I know my brother. He will — '

'Don't worry,' Isabelle said tightly. 'I know myself,
and I think I can handle your brother if he comes on
too strong.' She had been taught too hard a lesson by
Anthony when it came to fast-living, fast-loving men.
The only difference was that Jean-Luc Ferrat made no
bones about his woman-littered lifestyle, whereas
Anthony had hidden it until it was too late.

The helicopter was waiting for them on the side-
strip. It gleamed black in the sunlight as the officials

ushered them through, bowing low to Jean-Luc, who strode past them with a curt nod, a multi-millionaire used to his status and power, and the respect he commanded.

'Is this your first trip to Monaco?' Jean-Luc swung to look at her as he reached the aircraft.

'Yes,' she replied coolly.

A hard smile touched his mouth. 'Then sit beside me in the front. Your first glimpse of the principality will be superb.'

Isabelle had no choice but to obey, but as she slid into the co-pilot's seat she gave him a smile with her teeth bared and dislike flashing in her green eyes.

'All set?' Marie-Claire said, climbing into the back and slamming the door. '*On y va!*'

Jean-Luc slid the black leather head-set on, adjusting the microphone to his firm, sensual mouth. He started flicking switches, long fingers drawing the eye, the flash of a Rolex at his hair-roughened wrist as his white cuff shot back. Isabelle looked angrily away from his hands, prickling with dislike.

He was talking in cool, professional French to the control tower. The blades began to whirr overhead. The engines whined, flared, built to a low roar of power.

Suddenly, they were lifting off the ground into the hot blue sky.

'Where in America are you from, *mademoiselle*?' Jean-Luc asked above the engine noise.

'New Orleans.' Her Southern drawl leapt to the fore as she said the name with a sensual throaty sound that matched her long red-gold hair, slanting green eyes and slender, curvaceous body.

'Ah. . .' he murmured, and shot an admiring look

at her, smiling as he repeated it exactly as she had said it. 'New Orleans. . .'

'Have you ever been there?' she asked curtly, shifting.

'I drove across the United States when I was twenty-one.' He gave her a charming smile, his dark eyes seductive. 'It was quite an experience. Now I only go back there on business.' He steered out across the sea and the gleaming coast road, so beautiful from up here, the turquoise waters of the Mediterranean breaking on white sandy beaches, Spanish-style houses dotted in the hills and along the coast.

'I understand you run the Ferrat hotel empire,' Isabelle said, trying to keep the conversation as neutral as possible.

He inclined his dark head. 'Yes. What do you do, *mademoiselle*?'

'I'm a secretary.'

'Your French is quite superb.' He flicked a look at her through his jet-black lashes, smiling. 'Where did you learn it? I know New Orleans has a French flavour, but. . .'

'My father is French,' she said flatly. 'From Antibes.'

'Just down the coast from here? *Vraiment*?' The dark brows shot up. 'No wonder your accent is so pleasing to the ear! Southerners speak so differently from the gunfire French of Parisians.' His gaze shot to her ankles, caressing them, his mouth pursing. 'What made him move from Antibes to New Orleans?'

'He fell in love with my mother,' she said, and flicked her gaze from his to stare down at the rugged, sun-bleached cliffs below. Love on the rocks, she thought, seeing the sea crash over them. The chance for me to love has come and gone. I can't love if I no longer believe in it.

'A romantic story, *mademoiselle*. Are you a romantic woman?'

She looked at him, her mouth curling with dislike. 'Romantic? No, I'm not particularly romantic!'

'*Non*? You look romantic.' The dark eyes murmured, Come to bed, *chérie*, and let me make you feel romantic. 'Don't tell me — there are men dying of love for you in Paris. . .?'

'No,' she said shortly, folding her arms.

'Not even one?' His smile teased her sardonically.

'No!'

'*Dommage!*' he murmured. 'Well, if there were, they would have to forget you now, anyway, by turning to some other beautiful——'

'We don't all live according to your amoral code of conduct,' she said between her teeth.

He caught his breath sharply, staring.

She met his gaze with defiance. He was her host for the summer, and he no doubt thought her rude. But she had to make it clear to him that flirtation and false flattery would not work with her. In fact, no technique would work with her. Jean-Luc Ferrat might have a high success-rate with women, but he wasn't going to get anywhere with her — not even a quick, light flirtation on a sunny day. She was not interested in him, and he might as well know that now.

He seemed to get the message, his mouth tightening as he flew on, eyes narrowing, lapsing into silence.

Suddenly, the helicopter swung down like a black hornet over Monaco.

Isabelle gasped at the sight of it, spread out before her in hot sunlight — the crumbling medieval streets around the Prince's Palace, the ancient stone fortress

beside it, and the narrow, winding streets leading down
to the glitter, the glamour, the modern-day paradise
of Monte-Carlo with its harbour, its multi-million-
dollar yachts bobbing in the sunlight, and the sun-
bleached skyscrapers dotting the land below the rock.

Jean-Luc was talking in cool, clipped French, the
headphones crackling back with radio reports as he
gained clearance to land immediately at Fontvielle
Heliport.

'What do you think of your first sight of Monaco?'
Marie-Claire sat forward, her voice raised above the
engine noise as they swooped in.

'It's stunning!' Isabelle said. 'So much as I imagined
it. Is it really only two kilometres big?'

'One point nought eight miles square,' said Jean-
Luc tersely.

'Which bit is Monte-Carlo?' Isabelle asked, staring
down at the stunning sun-baked view.

'Oh, you're so American!' Marie-Claire laughed.
'Monte-Carlo is the whole of the ground area down
there. Yes, the modern part, with the yachts and
skyscrapers and our beautiful casino. Up here — this is
Monaco town, the old town, with the Prince's Palace
and the cathedral. And now we're landing at
Fontvielle; the new town. Prince Albert laid the first
stone in 1981, I think. Was it '81, Jean-Luc?'

'Yes,' Jean-Luc agreed, eyes narrowed as he let the
helicopter hover over the landing pad, sun-bleached
dust whirling up.

'Anyway, you'll love being here, I guarantee. Who
knows — you might even meet a gorgeous Monégasque
and fall madly in love!'

Isabelle gave an angry laugh. 'A man is the last thing
I want to find while I'm here! And besides — six weeks
is hardly long enough to fall in love with someone!'

'You don't believe in a *coup de foudre*?' Jean-Luc
drawled with a sudden re-emergence of that devastating charm. 'Love at first sight?'

'No,' she said pointedly. 'Love at first sight is just a
line playboys use to try and seduce women who are
stupid enough to believe them!'

The helicopter touched down. Two men in dark
suits ran to it as Jean-Luc Ferrrat took the head-set
off, flicked switches, then opened the door and
climbed out like a beautiful, dangerous wild animal.

'Take these cases,' he commanded one of the two
men, 'to my Ferrari.' Turning to the other, he said
curtly, 'Telephone ahead to let Raoul know I'll be late
for the meeting. Make sure he. . .'

Stepping out into the hot sunlight, Isabelle gazed in
wonder at the azure sea, the sun lilting on the ancient
buildings of Monaco, just across the cliff from them.
It was the most stunning view she had ever seen, all
that history, the streets so tiny, so crumbling, so pretty
in pink, and the ravishing glamour of Monte-Carlo
below. . .

'You're not getting on well with him, are you?'
Marie-Claire said softly beside her while Jean-Luc
continued giving a list of orders to his men.

'Oh, God, I'm so sorry, Marie-Claire,' she said, her
voice low. 'I keep trying to be friendly and polite,
but. . .' Her mouth twisted with bitter recognition of
her feelings. 'Maybe I should just leave!'

'No! I won't hear of it!' Marie-Claire was adamant.
'You need this vacation, you deserve it, and I'm going
to see that you get it!'

'I want to stay, but. . .' Isabelle's green eyes blazed
with sudden hatred. 'He's the last person in the world
I expected to meet here!'

'He's just treading on old wounds right now.'

'Yes. . .'

'But this will pass. He won't be around much, anyway.'

'I hope not,' Isabelle said tightly. 'Just the sight of him makes all my hackles rise!'

'How very inconvenient!' said a hard, angry voice above her head.

She spun, staring straight at his powerful chest.

There was a brief silence as they stared at each other. Isabelle raised her head, defiance flashing in her green eyes. It was just as well he had overheard that. Perhaps it would underline to him the reality of her feelings towards him. After all, he could hardly keep flirting with her if she made it as clear as day that she wasn't interested.

He looked furious, though. Angrier than he should have been, given that he barely knew her, and no doubt had millions of women just begging him to flirt with them.

'Come on!' he said tersely, swinging on his heel to stride away. 'I'll drive you both home and settle you in before I go to the board meeting.'

Marie-Claire and Isabelle exchanged wincing glances as they quickly followed him across Fontvieille Heliport to the car park, where his red Ferrari waited, the cases neatly stowed in the boot.

Isabelle got into the rear seat while Marie-Claire slipped into the front, beside her brother. His eyes moved angrily to the rear-view mirror as he started the car with a flare of smooth power. She looked away, aware that she had really offended him, and bitterly regretting it. If he hadn't flirted with her, let his eyes rove so insolently over her, she wouldn't have done it. His sexual appraisal of her had made her complexes rise up and snap at him like a nasty, hissing cat. She hated herself for it, but how could she possibly prevent it when he was everything that was so very dangerous to her?

Perhaps I should apologise to him, she thought suddenly. He is my host and Marie-Claire's brother, after all. I can hardly expect to spend the next six weeks as a guest in his apartment while I'm behaving like this — and it must be clear to him now that I'm not interested in him.

But her eyes were staring intently at his hand resting on the central console beside the auto-gearstick, and her mind was busy registering the black hairs growing over his strong wrist, the length of his fingers. . .

'Isn't it a beautiful day?' Marie-Claire said brightly.

'Mmm.' Jean-Luc let his angry gaze meet Isabelle's in the mirror.

The car was edging through the hot, crowded streets of Monte-Carlo, far below the palace cliffs and heli-port, past the harbour.

'Are you going out tonight, Jean-Luc?' Marie-Claire asked.

'Yes,' he said tersely, and reached out to switch the car CD player on, ending the conversation and flood-ing the luxurious interior with fast, hard, angry music.

The beat seemed to catch Isabelle's blood, making it throb as she studied Jean-Luc's tough face in the mirror, watching him hotly through her eyelashes, a dazed, intent expression in her green eyes as she felt them move to study his hard, sensual mouth and her whole body throbbed with fierce excitement at the thought of him kissing her. . .

He caught her.

Instantly, she dragged her gaze away, aware that her powerful desire had shown in her face.

He frowned, driving on, eyes narrowing then flicking

constantly from the road to the mirror, the road to the mirror. . .and then a slow, hard, sexy smile touched his mouth, a hot surge of recognition in his eyes as he met her gaze in the rear-view mirror and she felt her solar plexus jump.

Soon, the red Ferrari swung into a stone alley, driving down a slope that led to a small, private underground car park off a glittering, very expensive shopping street.

They all got out of the car. Isabelle avoided Jean-Luc's eyes, even though he gave her a long, hard, assessing stare, almost willing her to look up.

'Home at last!' Marie-Claire said brightly, trying to pretend there was not an atmosphere of tension between them all.

Jean-Luc strode ahead, jabbed the call button on the lift, and a second later they were all enclosed in its claustrophobic luxury, riding up to the top floor, and the penthouse apartment.

As the lift doors slid open, Jean-Luc was already striding ahead, across the polished parquet wood floor to the vast mahogany double doors which he unlocked deftly, and pushed open.

'Dusort!' he clipped out, striding into the apartment.

A man and woman hurried out to meet them. '*Oui, monsieur*? *Oh*! *Mademoiselle*! Welcome home, *ma petite*!'

Laughing, Marie-Claire went into the embrace of the fat dark-haired woman. '*Bon-bon*! Are you surprised? I told you I'd be back!'

'But so long in Paris, *chérie*!' The woman rolled her dark eyes. 'We thought you'd deserted your Monégasque roots for that awful city!'

Jean-Luc said, 'Look, I've got work to do. Dusort——' he threw his keys at the housekeeper's husband '—could you go down to the Ferrari? Their cases are in it. Bring them up and put them in their rooms.'

'*D'accord, monsieur*.' Dusort scurried to the door, smiling.

Isabelle stepped forward tensely. 'Monsieur Ferrat, I'd like to——'

'I'm going to my study, *mademoiselle*!' Jean-Luc said curtly. 'If you have anything to say to me, you may say it in there, in private!'

Turning on his heel, he strode away to a room off the luxurious hallway and slammed the door.

'Oh, dear!' Madame Dusort made a face, studying Isabelle. 'What have you done, *mademoiselle*, to make him slam doors like that?'

Isabelle felt her face grow hot. 'I was rather abrupt with him. I may have been too abrupt. I'm beginning to think I should go and apologise.'

'Oh, yes,' said the housekeeper, 'he likes it when people apologise. I should do that right away.'

Marie-Claire laughed at Isabelle's disconcerted expression. 'She's only pulling your leg, Isabelle! But you're right, an apology from you would certainly make him better-tempered.'

'Where will I find him?' Isabelle frowned. 'In there?'

'That's his study.' Madame Dusort nodded. 'But be careful to knock, and wait for him to say you can enter before you dare go in.'

'Stop exaggerating, you naughty thing! Is there any *chocolat-froid* in the fridge?' Marie-Claire led Madame Dusort away down the corridor.

Left alone in the expensive, beautifully decorated hallway, Isabelle studied the door to Jean-Luc Ferrat's study and quickly rehearsed what she would say before going to the door and knocking sharply on it.

'*Entrez*!' Jean-Luc called out.

Isabelle opened the door and slowly walked inside. There was a long, tense silence.

'Well, well, well,' he murmured, dark eyes narrowing.

Isabelle closed the door behind her and said coolly, 'I've come to apologise for my behaviour, *monsieur*. It was a difficult flight from Paris. I was tired and het up. I realise I was rude to you, but you must understand I have no wish to be flirted with. I'm here to spend time with your sister — not provide amusement for you when there are no other women around.'

'You're a very beautiful woman,' he drawled. 'I'm sure you're used to handling flirtatious men. Do you treat all of them as you treated me?'

'No,' she said without thinking. 'You're different!'

He sat forward, staring. 'Am I, indeed?'

'I didn't mean what you think I meant!' she snapped, colouring. 'Just that today was different. Because of the flight — the long journey. I wasn't in the mood to tolerate a flirtation. That's all.'

'Hmm.' The dark eyes flickered over her assessingly. 'Well, I'm afraid I don't accept that as your apology, *mademoiselle*. Perhaps you should start again.'

Silence. She felt the hairs on the back of her neck prickle.

'Monsieur Ferrat,' she said tightly, 'I really have no intention of making any other apology to ——'

'Then you're wasting my time.' He arched cool dark brows. 'And if you wish to remain under my roof in a civilised atmosphere, I suggest you go away and think about the real reasons for your behaviour. I'll be ready to accept an apology when I believe it's the truth. Until then, I don't think we really have anything more to say to each other.'

She just stood there, staring at him, speechless with confused rage.

He picked up a document from his desk and began studying it. Isabelle realised she had been dismissed. Her eyes blazed. 'That suits me fine, *monsieur*! In fact, I'd prefer it if we didn't have another conversation for the duration of my visit!' She turned on her heel and walked out. Slamming the door, she strode along the hallway, burning inside.

I'm not staying here, she thought, looking wildly around for a door that might tell her where the hell she should go. I can't possibly stay here. I've made a terrible mess of the whole trip. I'll have to pack up and go back to ——

'Isabelle!' Marie-Claire called in a sing-song voice from down the corridor. 'Come and have some *chocolat-froid*!'

Moistening her dry lips, she waited a few seconds before turning, suddenly realising that the hot sting of angry tears was in her eyes and not understanding why.

'Just coming!' she called with false gaiety, and forced a smile as she went to join Marie-Claire and Madame Dusort in the bright, modern kitchen. After all, she couldn't possibly drag Marie-Claire into this horrible mess by telling her how disastrous that interview had been.

CHAPTER TWO

WHAT did he mean, anyway? Isabelle wondered
furiously later as she stood on the balcony of her
bedroom, staring at the streets of Monte-Carlo, the
blue bay beyond, and the pink palace of the Grimaldis
perched on the cliffs above. My behaviour wasn't that
bad! OK, I was slightly rude. I said some cutting things
to him at the airport and in the helicopter, and then I
said something I shouldn't have said behind his back.
And to his sister, which made it worse, she had to
admit. But surely being tired and het-up was a good
explanation? Surely he couldn't just dismiss it like
that?

She sighed, and walked back into her bedroom. It
was beautiful, wide and airy and modernly French,
with a fan whirring overhead, a polished wood floor
strewn with luxurious rugs, and a vast double bed with
a pale pink duvet. Ornaments gleamed expensively on
antique tables. The long lace curtains at the balcony
windows swished softly in the hot breeze.

After the disastrous interview with Jean-Luc,
Isabelle had not told Marie-Claire anything—certainly
not how badly she had bungled it. It wouldn't have
been fair. Marie-Claire was her friend, the closest
friend she had had for a long, long time, and she loved
her very much.

'Did you soothe the savage beast?' Marie-Claire had
asked hopefully in the kitchen, and Isabelle had smiled
and replied that yes, she thought she had smoothed
things out between them.

24

But of course she had not soothed the savage beast at all. Far from it. In fact, she'd probably made him more savage than he was already. Her pulses leapt at the thought of another interview with him. What on earth would she say?

There was a sudden rap at her door.

'Come in!' she called distractedly.

The door opened. Her eyes widened in shock as she saw Jean-Luc Ferrat.

'You've settled in, then?' His face was cool, hard, expressionless, all anger gone, his mouth a firm line and his eyes hooded by those eyelids.

'I. . .' She felt her heart beat too fast. 'Yes, I'm very comfortable, thank you.'

'Good.' He slowly pushed the door shut.

Her heart beat even faster. 'What are you doing?'

'It's been over an hour since we last spoke,' he drawled with a lazy smile, and leaned against the door, drumming long fingers on the panels, watching her with his dark head bent, his eyes quite penetrating. 'I wondered if you had come to any conclusions about your behaviour.'

She stiffened angrily. 'Just that my explanation was perfectly reasonable!'

'Towards a man you've never met before?' His brows rose with cool mockery.

'I think so!' She folded her arms, deeply uncomfortable.

He straightened, walking towards her, a sardonic smile on his handsome mouth. Isabelle backed like a wary animal, her eyes very green. He stopped.

There was a little silence as he watched her with those clever dark eyes. 'You're still tired?' he drawled softly. 'After an hour's rest? Is that why you're backing away from me?'

'I'm alone in my bedroom with a man I don't know,' she said tensely, her whole body leaping with alarmed pulses. 'Of course I back away.'

'*Mademoiselle*,' he murmured with a cynical smile, 'I'm not only your host and your friend's brother — I am also Jean-Luc Ferrat, and I do not doubt for one second that you know my reputation with women.'

Her temper flashed like a rocket. 'Oh, I know your reputation!'

'And do you really think a man of my experience would be interested in sexual assault?'

'I wouldn't be remotely surprised, *monsieur*!' she said through her teeth, prickling from head to foot with angry hatred. 'In fact, nothing about the type of man you are would surprise me!'

'Ah. . . I was right, then,' he drawled, walking coolly towards her, a smile on his tough mouth.

'What's that supposed to mean?' She was backing rapidly. 'Hey!' She was breathless, her hands shooting up in self-defence. 'Get away from me! What do you think you're doing?'

'I don't know,' he murmured sardonically, towering over her, backing her up against the wall, his eyes glittering with sexual intent. 'What do you think I'm doing?'

'I. . .' She was dry-mouthed with panic. '*Monsieur*, don't stand so close to me; I. . .'

'And that's the real reason for your behaviour, isn't it?'

'No!' Her hands fluttered up in breathless panic.

'I'm attracted to you, too,' he murmured with a lazy smile, even closer now, his dark head bent. 'You don't have to fight me just because you want me to kiss you!'

She tried to get past him. 'No! I don't want you to do anything! Stay away from——'

'I think we'd better get this over with quickly,' he bit out, and pulled her suddenly into his arms, his dark head swooping as he heard her smothered gasp of angry pleasure just before his hard mouth closed burningly over hers.

Incoherent with rage and at the same time weak with desire, she struggled against him, her hands pushing at his chest and shoulders until he caught them and pinned them to her sides, his long hands firm but not painful on her wrists as he continued to kiss her, his mouth hot, experienced, demanding and insistent.

Her mouth was already opening, angry moans of resistance coming from the back of her throat, her body moving furiously every few seconds like the death throes of a gazelle in a lion's paws, but he held her fast, his mouth moving commandingly over hers, making her give hoarse, breathy moans of angry pleasure under the hot onslaught of his kiss.

His hard body was pressing against her, and she felt the heat in every nerve-ending until she was dizzy, dazed, breathless, her mouth passionate beneath his, lips swollen and bruised with the long, sexy kiss, and now she was very still in his arms, oblivious to anything but him.

Dazed, she felt his long hands releasing her wrists to move up her body.

As those long fingers closed over her breasts she gave an involuntary cry of hoarse pleasure, swaying under the onslaught of sheer sensuality, her hands going to his shoulders, then his neck; then, as her mind slipped completely from her grasp, she felt her fingers thrusting into his hair and her body arching against his with intolerable desire.

They were clinging together suddenly, and she was mindless, boneless, incapable of resisting as the wave of three years' frustration suddenly drowned her in a towering need for this, nothing but this, the hard mouth and hands and body of a man like Jean-Luc Ferrat, who was gorgeous, strong, powerful, sexy. . . She cried out hoarsely again and again at the delicious feel of his hard fingers on her full, aching breats.

'Isabelle!' Marie-Claire called from outside.

She opened her dazed eyes, breathing erratically, her heart pounding so loud she thought she might faint from the blood rushing around her already trembling body.

'Answer her quickly!' he muttered against her mouth. 'Tell her you'll be out in a minute!'

Flushed and weak at the knees, she stared up into his dangerous face and realised with horror the full impact of what had just happened between them.

'Answer her or she'll come in and find us,' he said thickly.

Breathless, she called in a ragged, uneven voice, 'I—I'll be out in a minute, Marie-Claire.'

'OK,' Marie-Claire called back. 'I'll be on the balcony.'

Jean-Luc lowered his dark head to recapture her mouth. She pushed him away, her eyes still dazed, whispering hoarsely, 'Get away from me.'

'Come on!' He pulled her back against him, his face darkly flushed. 'I thought we'd got past all that.'

'Past all what?'

'The pretence that you don't want me.' He arched dark brows, his voice husky, a sardonic smile on his tough mouth.

Her face ran angry red. 'I don't want you! And don't cite what happened just now as proof that I do. You cornered me and forced me to kiss you.'

'I didn't have to force you very hard!' he murmured

teasingly. 'And once we'd got past the forcing stage you were seriously responsive.'

'I was trapped! I ——'

'*Mademoiselle*, if my sister hadn't knocked on the door we'd have been on the bed by now, shedding clothes at a rate of knots.'

'We would not!'

'Let me kiss you again,' he drawled thickly, hands tightening on her, 'and we'll see if I'm right.' He bent his dark head, fire in his eyes.

'No! Get your hands off me and keep them off!' She slapped his face stingingly, making his head jerk back, anger flaring in his dark eyes as he stared down at her furiously. Isabelle stood her ground, saying with contempt, 'I detest men like you, and you're probably the most detestable of all your kind, you smooth, practised, phoney playboy!'

'OK, *chérie*,' he drawled tightly, releasing her, his teeth bared in an unpleasant smile as he stepped away and raked her from head to foot with angry eyes. 'If you're not prepared to admit you want me, I shan't waste any more time on you.' He turned and strode to the door, saying lazily over one broad shoulder, 'After all, there are plenty of women who'd jump at the chance to be in your shoes, getting thoroughly kissed by me.'

'Why, you conceited ——'

'Bastard?' He wrenched open the door, strode out, slamming it behind him.

Staring at the door with overwhelming hatred, she wanted to run after him and slap his arrogant face. She'd never seen conceit like it! My God, she thought savagely, how does he manage to walk with a head that big? I'm surprised he doesn't overbalance!

Tears stung her eyes suddenly. He might have made

a pass at her, but that was only because she was a woman. It had nothing to do with her, personally. He probably just thought it would be funny to toy with her. What had he said at the airport? 'The sad American girl. . .!' Yes, that was probably exactly what he thought of her: sad Isabelle, lonely and unloved, just ripe to fall into the skilled arms of a man like Jean-Luc Ferrat. And he felt so superior to her that he found it an amusing little game to come in here like that and kiss her.

Angry hurt stabbed at her heart. What hurt was the fact that she secretly thought he was the most gorgeous man she'd ever seen in her entire life — and to be approached seriously by him would be a dream come true.

The truth was, Jean-Luc Ferrat was just her type. Everything about him, from his looks to his lifestyle, that cool, clever mind, his sardonic sense of humour, his come-to-bed eyes, the Ferrari he drove and the helicopter he flew and even the way he moved his dark head, made her want to purr like a pussycat.

Once, Isabelle might have believed a man like him could want her.

But not now.

Not after Anthony.

She rubbed at her tears with a clenched fist, mouth trembling. Look what I've become, she thought angrily. A plaything to while away a few spare minutes. My first kiss in three long years, and it's just a joke to the man who gives it to me.

But at least the fact that it was her first kiss in three years helped explain her very feverish response to him. It was humiliating to remember how she'd clung to him like that, her mouth passionate and her body pressing against his in a manner she never thought she'd live to feel again. In fact — come to think of it — she'd never felt like that in her life before. But it can only be because I've been completely celibate for three years, she thought with a frown. After all, regardless of the horror of Anthony, we did occasionally make love, and once a woman's body has experienced physical pleasure it does crave it as a necessary part of life.

But who was she kidding? She had never felt physical pleasure! She had been such a hopeless lover, hopeless, totally inadequate. . .

Abruptly she got to her feet, her face tight. Don't think about it, she told herself fiercely. Just put the whole incident, and the past, out of your mind, and if Jean-Luc Ferrat comes near you again just slap him again and he'll leave you alone.

Determined, she went out of her bedroom, used to her loneliness and frustration and quite prepared to continue living with it rather than risk the kind of damage a man like Jean-Luc could do to her self-esteem ever, ever again.

Walking along the corridor, she found the door to the salon easily. It was a stunning room, with parquet floor, creamy sofas, an overhead fan, chandeliers and a ravishing selection of French antiques dotted around, all carved in gold oak.

The vast French doors opened on to a beige balcony of old stone, baking under the hot Mediterranean sun, a balustrade wall, and Marie-Claire herself sitting on a chair at a table.

'Hi!' Marie-Claire smiled as Isabelle stepped on to the hot balcony. 'What have you been up to all this time?'

'Oh, I just unpacked and settled into my room.' Isabelle went scarlet and stared across Monte-Carlo,

the clamour of traffic and people in the crowded streets
below a constant noisy cacophony of life.

'We'll be eating dinner at seven,' Marie-Claire said
lightly.

'That's fine — I'm not all that hungry anyway.' She
moistened her lips. 'Will your brother be eating with
us?'

'No, he's dining with a friend tonight.'

Isabelle felt angry, jealous disappointment. 'One of
his women?'

'Probably!' Marie-Claire laughed. 'I'm glad you're
getting on better with him, though.'

Isabelle flushed and looked away.

They spent an hour or so sitting on the balcony,
soaking up the sun, and discussing their plans for the
next few weeks.

'We're right in the middle of the International
Fireworks Festival here,' Marie-Claire told her. 'It's
really the loveliest display, right over the harbour, and
we'll go along to see that tonight.'

'Sounds great!' Isabelle said. 'But you said this was
the gala season — is anything else on while I'm here?'

'Oh!' She gave a Monégasque shrug, very sensual,
her shoulder curving. 'Galas here, parties there, con-
certs at the Prince's Palace.'

'A dizzy social whirl, then?'

'All leading up to the event of the year — the
Monégasque Red Cross Ball!' Marie-Claire's eyes glittered excitedly. 'You'll go to that, of course, with me
and my brother. We're invited every year, always have
been. It's wonderful. Celebrities, evening gowns, dia-
monds, paparazzi taking pictures everywhere. . .such
fun! And one of the few occasions when Jean-Luc
doesn't hate the paparazzi with a vengeance!'

Later, Isabelle went to her room to take a long

shower. She dried herself stealthily, disliking being
nude, and feeling angrily embarrassed by her naked
reflection in any mirror.

Then she dressed in a plain blue shift dress, struggling to tell herself she was pretty again, that her long
red-gold hair was OK like this, loose and sensual, and
that her make-up looked all right. She stood at the
mirror, fiddling anxiously with her appearance, adding
jewellery, taking it off, getting flustered, telling herself
angrily that she had to work at it, had to keep working
towards the girl she had once been so long ago in New
Orleans when everyone said she was a beauty. . .

Pain lit her green eyes. It was such a slow process.
She had worked so hard for so long, but still that final
piece of herself was not in place, still it was smashed
and beaten and defeated, hiding inside herself, and no
matter what she did she could not resurrect it.

In the end, she gave up and went out to find Marie-
Claire.

'What time will you be back?' Marie-Claire was
asking Jean-Luc in the salon as Isabelle went in.

'I don't know,' his deep, drawling voice replied.
'Late, I think.'

Her heart skipped furious beats at the sight of him.
He had showered and changed too, wearing a dark
blue suit, impeccably cut, his powerful body at ease as
he stood, hands in trouser pockets, radiating sex
appeal.

'Don't wait up for me. I might be —— ' He broke off,
seeing Isabelle, dark eyes racing over her as he drew
in his breath sharply, met her gaze, then ran a hand
through his dark hair, gave a cynical smile and
drawled, 'You look *ravissante, mademoiselle*!'

'Thank you,' she said tightly, and folded her arms,
her whole body stiffening with absolute rejection of

his admiration. 'It's seven o'clock, Marie-Claire. What time did you book the table for?'

'Seven-thirty. Will you give us a lift to the harbour, Jean-Luc?'

'Sure. Why not?' Jean-Luc looked across at Isabelle suddenly, an expression of resentment in his dark eyes. He had registered her rejection and it didn't please him any more than that slap had earlier. Isabelle's lashes flickered as she studied him, confused by his reactions to her. Why should he be remotely bothered if she accepted or rejected his advances? After all, he had more than enough women to keep him busy. As he had said himself, there were plenty who would give anything to be in her shoes, fighting Jean-Luc Ferrat off.

They took the lift down in an atmosphere of prickling tension that Marie-Claire must have been aware of, even as she chattered gaily about nothing in particular.

In the underground car park they approached the red Ferrari.

'Oh, no!' Marie-Claire said suddenly. 'My purse! I left it in my other bag! I'll have to go back!'

Jean-Luc leaned against the Ferrari like a living photograph. 'Go and get it, then. We'll wait for you here.'

Isabelle tensed, pulses racing at the thought of being alone with him again, but had to just stand there in silence as Marie-Claire's footsteps echoed back to the lift area.

In the cool, dimly lit car park, they looked at each other.

'Well, *chérie*,' he drawled suddenly, his smile cynical, 'is this how it's going to be between us? Hostility in public and passion in private?'

Her mouth tightened. 'There was no passion!'

'How can such a pretty mouth lie so much?' He strode coolly towards her, brows lifting as she backed at once. 'Backing away from me again? You only make me want you more by doing that. Don't you know that's not the way to keep me away from you?'

'Then tell me the way and I'll gladly use it!' she said insultingly, then gasped as her back hit a stone pillar and she was trapped.

'Be indifferent to me,' he said under his breath as his powerful body touched hers, trapping her effectively between him and the pillar. 'Don't jump every time you see me, don't snap at me angrily for no reason, and particularly—don't look at me with those sexy green eyes as though you are thinking how it would feel to make love with me!'

'I never looked at you like that! How dare you even suggest——?'

'*Chérie*——' he touched her hot throat with a long finger, making her shiver '—I'm thirty-six, and very experienced with women. I know when a woman is attracted to me. I can see it in her eyes as I see it in yours.'

'Don't be so insolent!'

'Then don't be so provocative.'

'I'm not!'

'Oh, yes,' he said tightly, and she could suddenly hear his heart thudding in his chest, 'you are intensely provocative! I don't think I've ever met a woman who looked at me with such blatant desire.'

That made her catch her breath, staring at him.

'When a hot look from a woman,' he said thickly, 'is combined with such a beautiful face and body—well, the truth is, Isabelle, I seem to find you quite irresistible.'

He's just trying to flatter you, she thought breathlessly, overwhelmed by the sudden flow of compliments from such a very desirable man.

'It's true.' He frowned suddenly, his voice deepening. 'Don't tell me you don't believe me? Surely you
must!'

She looked away angrily. 'I don't even remember
what you said! And kindly keep your empty compliments for the women who appreciate them. I'm not
one of them and I never will be!'

'That may be so,' he said flatly, 'but I can't stop
myself wanting to change your mind. I may as well be
frank, because if you're staying here for the summer
I'm not going to be able to keep my hands off you,
and——'

'Look, just forget it!' she shouted angrily. 'I have no
intention of joining your infamous list!'

He nodded slowly, his mouth tightening as he drew
an angry breath. 'There it is again. You really are
aware of my reputation, aren't you?'

Suddenly, that serious note in his voice took them
down like a lift to a lower floor, a deeper floor, one
that alarmed Isabelle even more than his very effective
seduction technique. There was an intimacy in it that
scared her.

'Yes, I am aware of your reputation,' she said in an
unsteady voice. 'I should think every woman you ever
meet is aware of it!'

'Some of them love it while others hate it,' he said
flatly. 'But I've never met a woman who did both.
Certainly not in such powerful extremes as you. You're
almost incoherent at both ends of the scale. I seem to
affect you more than any other woman I've met. But
why is that? Why, when——?'

'Your conceit is becoming a joke,' she said fiercely,

afraid of what he was going to say next. 'I don't love or hate your reputation! I despise it. Now, just leave me alone, you phoney third-rate playboy!'

'I may be a playboy,' he bit out in a voice like a whiplash, 'but I am not a phoney and certainly not third-rate — or have you forgotten your very passionate response to my kiss this afternoon in your bedroom?'

Isabelle lowered her gaze at once, breathless and angry but unable to reply, hating him for reminding her of her own traitorous response to him.

He studied her bent head with hard, narrowed eyes. 'Look — I'm doing my best to find out exactly why I'm caught up in a battlefied with you. I have no intention of taking all your missiles head-on, or keeping away from you in order to maintain an armed truce. I want you, as I have already made clear, and I know damned well that you want me. But whatever happens between us will not contain any further outbursts of gross disrespect from you. If you ever speak to me like that again, I'll give you a taste of my anger that you won't forget — am I making myself clear?'

'Yes!' she said tightly, hating him.

'Good.' He watched her still, eyes narrowed. 'And look at me when I'm slapping your wrist.'

She looked at him with rage, hatred, fear, respect and desire.

He exhaled thickly. 'My God. . .' his hard mouth parted as he stared into her blazing eyes '. . . I've never met anything like you before! What the hell is going on inside that beautiful head when you look at me like that?'

There was a long, tense silence. He studied her, his eyes narrowing with intense fascination and quick, clever thought, a frown drawing his dark brows together as his mind moved rapidly to a conclusion of some sort about her, one she knew she would definitely not like.

'Hang on. . .' he said under his breath. 'I've got it. I remind you of someone else. Someone who left you with some nasty scars. Really nasty scars, nasty enough for you to want to scratch my eyes out as soon as look me in the face.' He nodded slowly, seeing her appalled expression. 'That's it, isn't it? I'm paying somebody else's backbill.'

She couldn't speak, just stared at him in shock, the truth of what he'd guessed revealed in her eyes. She felt suddenly more vulnerable than she had in years, and hated him even more for it, staring into his dark eyes and seeing a sudden deep interest in her, in her self, in her battered heart that terrified her.

Footsteps clattered into the car park suddenly.

'Sorry I took so long!' called Marie-Claire, clattering under the dim lighting. 'I couldn't find it anywhere!'

Jean-Luc had already straightened, turned, and was striding coolly to the car with that predatory masculine grace. 'But you're ready to leave now? Then let's go!'

Monte-Carlo was alive with people, all thronging through the streets as the sun turned gold above the casino's green turrets, and nightlife began slowly to warm up, anticipating the hot, glamorous darkness.

He dropped them at the harbour. 'Have a good evening.' He kissed Marie-Claire on each cheek, then drawled softly. 'A kiss, Isabelle, for your host.'

She froze in the back, her hand on the door-handle.

Marie-Caire got out of the car, smiling, and waited on the pavement.

'One kiss,' murmured Jean-Luc, watching her, his dark head leaning back against the head-rest of the driver's seat, waiting. . .

Angrily aware of her own peculiar pleasure, she

leaned forward and brushed her mouth softly against his hard, bruised-looking cheekbone.

He caught her wrist in long fingers. 'What time do you think you'll be home tonight?'

'I don't know,' she said under her breath. 'Why?'

'Try to get in before midnight,' he murmured, kissed her wrist, released her hand, then sat forward, revving the engine as she slowly got out of the car.

As the door closed, he was already driving away, red racing tail-lights flaring. Isabelle stared after the car in bewilderment. What on earth had he meant by that? And why had he suddenly changed from an inquisitor to a seducer again, getting her to kiss him like that, asking her what time she would be home. . .?

'You *are* getting on better together, aren't you?' Marie-Claire giggled beside her, and gave her a teasing shove.

Isabelle pretended casual laughter, but it was unsteady; in fact she was beginning to feel very unsteady about this whole holiday now that Jean-Luc Ferrat was showing such interest in her. But why was he interested? Why? A man like that—he must have hundreds of women. And who was she in comparison with Europe's top beauties? Nobody, she thought bitterly as she walked with Marie-Claire across the Quai des Etats-Unis. He's just toying with me because he's got nothing better to do.

They ate at an Italian restaurant on the harbour, watching the sun set over the bay, the warm air delightful and the lights going on across Monte-Carlo reminding Isabelle of glamorous cities all over the world. As Italy was only half an hour's drive down the coast, there were a lot of Italian restaurants in the principality, and also as many Italians as Monégasques living here. In fact, the largest chunk of the population were French, although residency was very hard to establish, and people from all over the world clamoured to live in this beautiful principality, only two kilometres square, because of its tax advantages, its crime-free streets and, of course, its breathtaking glamour.

Later, when the fireworks exploded over the bay, Isabelle gasped in delight as the multicoloured light and noise burst in five, six, seven huge firework pom-poms of red, white, yellow, blue, gold, green. . .

'Oh, how beautiful!' she said, her face reflecting the colours.

'I know!' Marie-Caire laughed. 'And I never get used to it, even after a lifetime. All the world's leading firework manufacturers take part. Every year, something new, something more dazzling. . .'

They got home at eleven o'clock.

'I'm so sleepy. . .' yawned Marie-Claire as they entered the apartment's impressive hallway. 'Would you mind if I went to bed?'

'Of course not. I'm exhausted too. All that travelling.'

Marie-Claire hesitated at her bedroom door. 'You like it here? You don't miss Paris?'

'Where?' Isabelle laughed softly, and went into her bedroom, saying goodnight.

She got undressed, slipping into her cream cotton nightdress and cleaning her teeth, brushing her long red-gold hair, yawning as she finally went into the bedroom and slid into the large pink double bed.

If Jean-Luc had expected to find her awake at midnight waiting for him, he was in for a surprise, she thought, feeling her eyes close with tiredness and her mind begin to relax in sleep.

But he was waiting for her in her dream. . . It began slowly.

She was in New Orleans, standing at the attic window, staring out at the steamy heat, suddenly aware that it was cold in the attic, so cold, and that she was shivering uncontrollably.

Someone knocked on the attic door. Isabelle opened it. Jean-Luc came in and pointed to a big red trunk in the corner of the attic. She gasped as she realised it was her trunk, full of all her old clothes from when she was twenty-one, the belle of her home town, admired and loved by everyone she knew.

Isabelle went to the trunk and tried to open it, but realised it was locked and started to cry. 'My clothes, my clothes, my beautiful clothes. . .'

'I'll open it for you,' Jean-Luc Ferrat said, and she was suddenly in his arms, kissing him, burning hot, her skin almost on fire, so hot, so hot, so hot. . .

They were on the floor suddenly, crying out with excitement, and she was pushing his shirt off, burying her face in his hard male chest and saying urgently, 'I want you, I need this. . .my body needs it. . .'

She woke up gradually, the hot darkness all around her, and Jean-Luc's mouth on hers, his harsh breathing and fierce heartbeat terribly real as he kissed her with deep hunger, his strong hands moving over her breasts, fondling them below the cotton nightdress.

This was no dream. This was real.

Her eyes were open and the room swam as she said hoarsely, 'Get your hands off me, you swine! Oh, God, get off me. . .!' She started to fight him, crying out in panic.

He dragged his hot mouth from hers, darkly flushed, and held up his strong hands, saying thickly, teasingly, smiling unsteadily, 'All right, all right — look; no hands!'

Isabelle clutched the duvet to her breasts, shaking. 'What the hell are you doing in my bedroom?'

CHAPTER THREE

'KISSING you, Isabelle,' he drawled, breathing hard, looming over her with glittering eyes, his heart banging audibly. 'What do you think I'm doing in your bedroom?'

His black waistcoat was unbuttoned and hanging loose around his powerful torso, the white shirt unbuttoned to reveal the kind of chest that made her toes curl and her temperature rocket. He wore no jacket, and his tie was coiled like a slim black serpent on the duvet between them.

'Well, you can just stop!' she said tightly, her pulses roaring in her ears. 'My God, this is exactly what I'd expect from you! Sneaking in here to seduce me in my sleep! You ought to be ashamed of yourself!'

'I have a beautiful woman staying in my home and I want to make love to her. Why shouldn't I sneak into her bedroom at night and kiss her?'

'Because you've just been out all night with another woman!' Her fierce voice spat with contempt.

There was a brief silence. Jean-Luc watched her from below half-closed lids, his eyes shuttered and unreadable. Then he gave a lazy smile and drawled, 'She is just a friend.'

'Just a friend?' Isabelle's eyes burned with hatred. 'You really make me sick. Don't tell me you've been talking platonically to her all night long, or I'll slap your face.'

'How very passionate of you,' he murmured teasingly. 'But I should tell you it's only one o'clock. I've hardly been out with her all night.'

'I'm sure that wouldn't stop you! I know just what a fast worker you are!'

He laughed under his breath.

'Is she a blonde?' Isabelle asked, twisting the knife into herself. 'Or a brunette?'

The dark lashes flickered, then he said softly, 'She is blonde, but she is just a friend, and I didn't come here to talk about her.' His eyes grew gentle as he added deeply, 'I haven't forgotten what you inadvertently revealed to me tonight when we spoke in the car park.'

Isabelle stiffened, eyes lowering from his gaze.

'I was right, wasn't I?' Jean-Luc said, touching her cheek with one strong hand. 'I am paying somebody else's bill.'

She kept her eyes hidden, angry colour flooding her skin, her hands clenching into fists as she clutched the duvet to her neck.

'Some other man,' he said, watching her, 'who affected you so deeply that you can't even look at me without wanting to scratch my face to ribbons in revenge.'

'I don't want to talk about it,' she said thickly.

'Who was he? What was his name and where did you meet —— ?'

'Mind your own business!'

'Did he look like me? Is that it?'

'Look, you have no right to do this,' she said under her breath. 'I barely know you! I only met you this morning! Who the hell do you think you are, coming here like this, trying to force me to —— ?'

'I think I'm a man who wants to take you to bed but has a number of obstacles in his way,' he drawled sardonically. 'And there's only one way to deal with obstacles — remove them. This man in your past is the central obstacle, is he not? Then I wish to remove him. It's as simple as that.'

'As simple as that. . .' she repeated through her teeth, temper making her heart beat angrily.

'So.' His eyes glittered with mockery. 'What was his name, did he look like me, and when did you last see him?'

Isabelle studied him in the darkness for a long time, breathing hard.

'Tell me, Isabelle,' he murmured, 'or I'll start to kiss you again, and I won't stop until you tell me what I want to know.'

She trembled with furious, excited fear, hating him, deeply aware that if he started to kiss her she would go up in flames, her pulses already racing as she struggled to avoid looking at that sexy, male chest of his.

'His name was Anthony,' she said in a low, angry rush.

'Did he look like me?'

'No, he was blond and not as tall as you. I last saw him in New Orleans three years ago.'

'Is that why you went to Paris? To get away from bad memories?'

Isabelle glared at him in silence, feeling the hot prick of angry tears, hating him for seeing so easily the deepest roots of her intense vulnerability and pain.

'We all have bad memories, Isabelle,' he said deeply. 'But locking them up keeps them bad. You should take this opportunity to share them with me. It will help you recover.'

'I don't need to recover,' she said between her teeth. 'I know exactly what happened, and I'm certainly not about to discuss it with you! Now get out of my room and stay out, you phoney two-bit Casanova!'

His hands caught her shoulders as anger leapt in his eyes and he pushed her back against the pillows. 'Two-bit, *chérie*? I think not! Let's take it one more time from the top — you just stop me when you're so dizzy you can't think straight any more!'

She moaned furiously as his hot mouth closed over hers in a fierce kiss that sent her blood-pressure rocketing even as she struggled, making hoarse sounds of resistance against his masterful and very commanding mouth, hearing her heart banging as loud as his, her hands pushing at his shoulders, pushing, pushing. . .and suddenly sliding with a low groan of desire to his black hair, caressing him, arching with terrible excitement as his strong hands closed over her breasts, long fingers expertly stroking to give maximum pleasure.

'Dizzy yet, *chérie*?' He was breathing roughly, his heart banging. 'Hmm?' His hands tightened on her breasts. 'Ah, yes. . .!'

Her dazed eyes opened. Appalled, she dashed his hands away, hatred in her horrified exclamation. 'You're just an expert when it comes to seduction!'

Jean-Luc drew back, smiling sardonically, his heart thudding hard in his bare chest as he looked down at her with triumph in his dark eyes. 'Not two-bit, then? How rapidly you change your mind.'

'You know how to make a woman respond,' she said shakily, hatred in her eyes, 'and you're probably the best kisser I've ever met, but I don't *want* to be kissed by you, because I know it's just a skill you taught yourself — a skill you've practised on thousands of women!'

'Hardly thousands,' he drawled, laughing under his breath.

'Hundreds, then.'

He arched dark brows, a sardonic smile on his tough mouth.

'You don't deny it, I see!'

'Isabelle, it has nothing to do with my interest in you.'

'You're not interested in me,' she said bitterly, 'you just fancy seducing me! That's not the same thing.'

'On the contrary, I'm intoxicated by you. Fascinated, even.'

She stared, heart banging hard. 'Don't exaggerate. . .'

'*Chérie*, I've never met such a mystery as you, and I am more than fascinated. In fact, I warn you now—I intend to unwrap you like a Christmas present before you leave this principality.' He smiled, drawled softly, 'Have dinner with me tomorrow night at the Hôtel de Paris.'

'What. . .?' She stared, incredulous for a second that he should want to have dinner with her. Then she remembered it was all just part of his seduction technique, and her hurt made her say fiercely, 'Go to hell! I'm not joining your legendary list of conquests!'

'No, you're going straight to the top of the mystery list!'

'What mystery? There is no mystery! I just don't want to be seduced by——'

'But that is the very centre of it.' His voice made that sudden switch to deep intimacy that had unnerved and alarmed her earlier tonight when they'd spoken in the car park. 'You *do* want to be seduced by me. You want it more than any woman I've ever met.'

'No——' She tried to sit up, her face burning.

He held her beneath him, saying deeply, 'You insult me, push me away, shout at me, say you want to slap my face — and then burn up like a forest fire the minute I start to kiss you.'

'No, I don't — it's you, your skill, your experience with women, that's all!'

'No, Isabelle. It's personal. You want *me*, not my skill. Your desire is even more powerful than your hatred. I'm beginning to think you might actually faint with pleasure as I take you.'

'Oh. . .! You conceited, arrogant ——'

'With that in mind,' he drawled sardonically, 'I've come here to deliver an ultimatum. Either you agree to have dinner with me tomorow night or I exercise the considerable power I have over you — and really turn the heat up.' His dark brows arched as he murmured, 'You'd be a landslide, *chérie*. One kiss and ——'

'I'd stop you before you got further than a kiss.'

'You think?'

'I know!'

'Shall we put it to the test?'

Isabelle stared into his handsome face and knew she would never be able to stop him, not if he turned the heat up, not if he really opened up that channel of desire blazing between them.

'Very well, then,' he said softly, lowering his dark head.

'No!' Her hands came up in angry alarm. 'All right. If it's so important to you, I'll have dinner with you. But it won't get you anywhere. I won't tell you a thing about myself, and I certainly will not allow you to kiss or touch me as you have done tonight.'

'In the Salle Empire of the Hôtel de Paris?' he

drawled, a lazy smile on his hard mouth. 'We would shock all of Monaco!'

'You know very well what I meant!'

'Ah, yes, but do you?' he murmured, arching dark brows. There was a brief silence, then he got to his feet, picking up his tie from the bed. 'I forgot to tell you, when you woke up, how skilfully you had undressed me. I don't suppose you remember where you put my jacket when you tore it from me?'

Her breath caught in horror. 'What. . .? I — I don't believe you!'

'Ah. . .there it is!' The dark eyes glinted as he bent to retrieve it from the floor. 'You really are a very passionate woman. I particularly liked the way you unbuttoned my waistcoat, saying, "I need your body, I need it, I need——"'

'Oh, no. . .!' Her hands flew to her face in horror.

He watched her in the darkness, then said deeply, 'You're shocked and afraid, *chérie*. But you needn't be. I understand better than you know what it is to live with sexual frustration, and——'

'Shut up!'

'And tomorrow night,' he went on, buttoning his shirt with long fingers, 'I will question you closely as to why you have been living with it for so long. You find it difficult, hmm? Not surprising — a woman as desirable as you. But you need to end it. That much is clear. And I have every intention of helping you.'

'Get out!' Her voice shook with fury. 'I've changed my mind! I won't have dinner with——'

'I will not take you tomorrow night,' he murmured, and bent his dark head to kiss her gently. 'But I will question you over dinner. And I want my questions answered. Be prepared to tell me the truth — or I will force it out of you, *chérie*, with all the skill at my disposal.'

She just stared at him, incapable of speech.

'*A demain, chérie*!' he said under his breath, walking to the door, his jacket slung coolly over one broad shoulder. 'Eight o'clock at the Hôtel de Paris.' He opened the door, murmured, '*Faites de beaux rèves*. . .' and was gone.

For a long time after the door closed she just sat there, rigid with horror at her own wanton behaviour. How could she have pushed his clothes off in her sleep without knowing it?

It was because she had been dreaming when he came into the bedroom. That stupid dream! It was all she could remember of her appallingly wanton behaviour — just the closing moments of that dream. And in it, she knew, she had pushed at Jean-Luc's clothes, burning with frantic desire, needing to feel his flesh against hers, needing to feel his body inside hers to make her whole, needing it. . .

But it had not just been desire that triggered that dream.

Isabelle thought back to the beginning of the dream, aware that it had begun with a feeling of deep trust and understanding. Jean-Luc said in real life that he wanted to solve the mystery she presented him with. Well, wasn't that exactly what the dream had been telling her? That he was the only man she had ever met who *could* help her solve the mystery? And she was a mystery, even she knew that. Locked up, layered in hurt and lack of confidence, but yearning to be free, yearning to love and be loved. . .and to make love with a man, one man, *only* one. In a moment of sudden stark self-awareness, she felt a piece of herself flying back from the grave of shattered self-esteem, and knew she was a one-man woman, wandering like a ghost through Paris, crying silently inside for the loss of love, the ruined belief in love, the inability to be anything other than what she had been all along. A one-man woman.

And now, it seemed, she had met that one man.

She put her hands to her face, appalled. Denial raged inside her. He can't be the one man, she thought fiercely. I refuse to let him be. Not him, not Jean-Luc Ferrat, a notorious womaniser who'll take my battered heart and break it into tiny pieces. Yet still she could not deny the ferocious desire burning within her for a touch of his hand, the feel of his mouth on hers, and the way she had pushed his clothes off tonight, needing to see and feel and taste his skin.

No wonder he had said he would exercise his 'considerable power' over her! And he must have known she was asleep, dreaming—he must have known, or why had he stopped kissing her when she woke up and realised what was happening? Because he wanted to ask me those very astute questions about Anthony and my past in New Orleans. . .

This man is much faster and cleverer than me, she thought with sudden shock. He's been ten steps ahead of me from the word go. He's taken every confusing statement I've thrown at him and read the truth behind it. What was he—a bloody mind reader? How could he possibly guess that beneath her hatred and fury lay such boiling desire?

And more. . .some dangerous emotional reaction that she as yet did not fully understand. I don't want it, she thought in angry fear. I won't feel it and I won't let him anywhere near me, ever again.

But he had just forced her to have dinner with him tomorrow. . .

* * *

Next day, she joined Marie-Claire for breakfast on the hot balcony. A pot of fresh coffee, a basket of croissants, *petits pains au chocolat* and warm brioches, all baked here in Monaco.

'Jean-Luc's gone to work.'

'Oh?' Isabelle bit into a croissant indifferently, but she felt her heart skip beats just at the sound of his name.

'He tells me you're having dinner with him tonight at the Hôtel de Paris?'

She flushed, sipped her café crème. 'Oh, yes. . . I hope you don't mind, Marie-Claire. I'm supposed to be here with you after all, and——'

'No, no! It'll give me a chance to catch up with some of my old friends.' Marie-Claire smiled. 'Zooming around in a convoy of fast cars and loud music—beep-beep!'

Isabelle laughed, relaxing. 'You're going out tonight too, then?'

'We're all going to Jimmy'z—the Régine night-club—to dance the night away and be young, single Monégasque babes.'

'That sounds like fun!'

'Oh, it will be! But what about today? What shall we do together on your first morning in Monaco?'

Isabelle sighed deeply. 'Oh, I'd love to see the palace. . .!'

An hour later, she was standing in front of it. The beige-pink walls were creamily lit by hot sunlight, smooth and tranquil as a lifesize doll's palace, the rock looming behind its toytown battlements, the long rows of arched windows hiding the mysteries at the heart of its historic presence in Europe, and two candy-striped sentry boxes standing either side of the carved stone doorway with the Grimaldi crest above it.

Here the legend had begun in the thirteenth century, when François 'Malizia' Grimaldi had seized the fortress by disguising himself as a monk and murdering the guard. The event was commemorated on the Grimaldi coat of arms with two monks holding a sword.

Over seven centuries his descendants had ruled here, sometimes in peace, sometimes chaos, but always with the name Grimaldi stamped firmly into the rock of Monaco. Their names littered Monégasque history with glamour and tragedy as they passed the principality down through the ages. Honoré II, the first Prince of Monaco in 1612. His son, Antoine, the first getter of glamour by marrying Marie de Lorraine of the royal house of France. Florestan I, who struggled throughout his reign to keep the lands of Menton and Roquebrune under Monégasque rule. His son Charles III who finally ceded the rights to those towns in 1861, and found Monaco facing financial disaster unless action was taken to guard the last two kilometres left of the once-large principality. Charles III and his beautiful mother, the first Princess Caroline, had hit on the brilliant idea of building a vast casino — the Société des Bains de Mer — and thus saved the principality from bankruptcy.

'It's all thanks to Charles III,' Marie-Claire told her as they sat at a café in the sunlit palace square. 'He founded the casino in 1863, and saved us from ruin. Overnight, Monaco became the most popular place on the Riviera — and in 1866 we named the town after him: Monte-Carlo.'

'It's one of the most famous towns in the world——' Isabelle sipped her ice-cold Perrier ' — and its name is just the epitome of glamour.'

'Especially since our beloved Princess Grace married Rainier in 1956. Oh. . .what a day that must have been here!' Marie-Claire's eyes saddened. 'We miss her so very much. She was deeply loved.'

'Princess Stéphanie was in the car with her, wasn't she——' Isabelle studied the creamy palace walls '—when she had that fatal crash in '82?'

'Poor Stéphanie.' Marie-Claire winced in sympathy. 'It must have been horrific. But the family are said to have a curse on them.'

'Really?' Isabelle looked at her with interest.

'Yes, a medieval Grimaldi offended a witch and she placed a curse on them—that no Grimaldi would ever have a happy marriage.'

Isabelle thought of Princess Caroline, and of the accident which had so cruelly robbed her of the man she had loved. 'Do you believe it's true?' she asked, shivering. 'There have been so many tragedies. . .'

'No, it's just a silly superstition. Tragedy colours everyone's life at some point or another. We just don't have the Press waiting like vultures to catch a glimpse of our grief.' Marie-Claire's eyes flashed angrily. 'I think that must be the true curse of the Grimaldis.'

Later, they walked back down the cobbled medieval streets of Monaco town, crammed with sun-bleached crumbling buildings, souvenir shops, cafés, antique and bric-à-brac shops.

'Send a postcard home,' Marie-Claire suggested suddenly. 'To your famille in *les Etats-Unis*.'

Isabelle's face paled. 'No. Another day, perhaps.'

'You can't keep on just contacting them at Christmas, Isabelle. They are your family, *chérie*, however hurt they have made you feel. But let's not get serious! We are young and in Monaco—shall we go to the Beach Club? Swim, sunbathe, wet-bike— beep-beep!'

They spent the rest of the day at the exclusive Monte-Carlo Beach Club. By the time they got home they were both sun-flushed, and Isabelle's nerves were growing more and more tense about tonight.

'What is this Hôtel de Paris and what should I wear?' she asked.

'It is the most famous and opulent hotel in Monte-Carlo,' Marie-Claire told her. 'Every crowned head in Europe must have stayed there since it was built last century. You must wear a stunning evening gown, Isabelle, and look glamorous for Jean-Luc!'

Nothing could have alarmed her more.

Glamorous, she thought bitterly as she went into the bathroom and took a quick shower. How am I supposed to look glamorous when I can only just find the strength to tell myself I'm pretty?

Hunting through her wardrobe, she tried on seven different dresses in growing frustration. Nothing looked good, let alone glamorous. She eventually chose a black strapless dress, knee-length and simple. Then she brushed her long red-gold hair in the loose style she preferred, added a touch of make-up, thrust her feet into high heels and looked around the room for her evening bag.

Suddenly, waves of *déjà vu* swept over her.

The heat through the open French balcony doors, the fan whirring overhead, the stylish antiques in the room. . .it was as though she were back in New Orleans in the old days, the golden days.

That's over, she thought bitterly, picking up her bag from the bed. I'll never be that girl again, and I'll never go back to New Orleans, not ever.

Isabelle walked out of the room, said goodbye to Marie-Claire, then made her way to the Hôtel de Paris, only two short streets away in the Place du

Casino. It was a lovely, warm, sunlit evening and the
usual stream of Bentleys, Rolls-Royces and red-
blooded Ferraris were edging through the streets with
glamorous people driving them.

The Place du Casino was the heart of Monte Carlo,
the gardens lush and green, fountains spraying, palm
trees waving softly against a hot blue-gold sky, and the
Hôtel de Paris a monument to elegance, grandeur and
opulence. Art nouveau carriage-lamps stood below
white stone steps, gold canopies across gleaming doors
and arched windows.

Isabelle went up the steps, head held high, and
entered the air-conditioned luxury hotel with its soaring ceilings, chandeliers and ambience of hushed,
exclusive turn-of-the century grandeur.

Suddenly her heart jumped as though hit by a
nuclear warhead.

Jean-Luc Ferrat was leaning coolly in a shadowy
alcove with a stunning blonde, one strong hand on her
chin as he lifted her beautiful face for a kiss. Jealousy
stabbed her savagely. She felt herself shake with it,
hating him violently, and feeling utterly inferior to the
elegant blonde.

Isabelle turned angrily and walked away, smarting
under her icy dignity as she made her way to the world-
famous Salle Empire.

An elegant and polite waiter seated her at a table in
the formal dining-room. She ordered a kir royale and
sat waiting angrily amid the gilded pillars, cathedral
arches and beautiful chandeliers.

Jean-Luc strode in suddenly, looking gorgeous in a
dark grey business suit with red silk tie and gold watch-
chain. He looked like a lean muscled animal, his hair
gypsy-black and his eyes glittering.

'*Chérie*,' he said as he reached her, 'you're early. Or

am I late?' He glanced at the Rolex on his wrist as he rested one strong hand on the back of her chair, leaning over her. 'No — you're early.' He bent his dark head, kissed her cheek, said with a come-to-bed smile, 'Did you have a good day? You look quite mouth-watering in that dress. . .'

'How very flattering you are, *monsieur!*' she said tightly, hatred in her green eyes. 'Another of your skills with women?'

'You wouldn't hate me so much,' he drawled sardonically, 'if you knew how much I've been thinking of you today.'

'I'm sure I can guess what you were thinking!' she snapped angrily.

'Bet you can't.' He flashed wicked dark eyes at her.

She felt breathless, light-headed. 'After your — your behaviour since I arrived in Monaco,' she stammered, 'I think I can guess all too easily!'

He laughed under his breath. 'You'd be more shocked than you could possibly imagine!' He moved to the elegant chair opposite her and sank down. 'You should never take for granted, *chérie*, what other people are thinking. And never, ever judge a book by its cover.'

'I think the cover of your particular book, *monsieur*, is one I know intimately!'

'Oh, you've been thinking about me too, have you?' he drawled, studying her full breasts beneath the black silk dress, and seeing her nipples erect with a sudden fierce desire that made his breath quicken as he lifted dark eyes to hers. 'Ah, yes. . . I see that you have.'

She was saved from answering that because the *maître d'* swept up to take their order personally, deferential to Jean-Luc, his obvious respect underlining Jean-Luc's power and authority. The memory of his commanding mouth on hers made her pulses leap with angry excitement at the thought of what was to come tonight. She hated herself for it, knowing he had other women, the way he had kissed that blonde making her veins sing with jealous pain. He had said the woman was just a friend — who was he kidding? They were clearly more than friends.

'So,' he drawled, sipping his wine when they were alone, 'where did you get your undeniable good taste and European manners?'

Her eyes flashed. 'I have no intention of answering any of your questions, *monsieur* — particularly when they come liberally peppered with your smooth, con-man Casanova flattery!'

His mouth tightened. 'Any more insults from you, Isabelle, and I won't just kiss you when we get home.'

Breathless with rage, she just glared at him, her heart banging loudly and her body tense as a bowstring from neck to ankles.

A hard smile twisted his mouth. 'And don't dare me, because I'd leap at the chance!'

Hatred shimmered like green fire in her eyes.

'Now,' he said under his breath, 'put your hostility away. We are on neutral ground — and we have no option but to talk.'

'I don't want to talk!' she choked out thickly.

'But I do. I want to find out all about you. So tell me what I wish to know, or let my imagination run riot about what I'm going to do to you when we get home.'

Her pulses leapt like firecrackers and she said in a hot rush, 'All right, what do you want to know?'

'So obedient,' he mocked softly, leaning back, running one long finger slowly over his hard, sardonic mouth. 'Tell me about your whole life before you met me. That's what I want to know.'

'I told you I was born and bred in New Orleans. My father is French, my mother Amnerican, and New Orleans is very French-influenced, too, which may account for the fact that I'm not just bilingual, but bi-national.'

'Hmm.' He studied her with thoughtful eyes. 'There's something about you that makes me believe you come from an excellent family. Is that the case?'

Surprise made her stare, her lips parted.

'Yes?' His dark brows rose.

'Yes. . .' She was staring, thinking, Nobody's said that to me since I left New Orleans.

'Your father is French, you say. I'd guess he was also wealthy?'

'Yes. . .' Her voice was husky, so she cleared her throat and forced it to sound cool and strong, lifting her red head. 'He's very powerful in New Orleans, and very wealthy.'

'And your mother?'

'Her parents own the biggest plantation in Louisiana, and can trace their roots back to the eighteenth century.'

His hard mouth twisted in a cool smile. 'A true Southern belle, then?'

'Oh, yes. . .she is!'

'I meant you, Isabelle.'

She paused, feeling foolish, then said tightly, 'Of course.'

Their meal arrived. The old chandeliers gleamed soft gold under the soaring cathedral arches of the magnificent dining-room. Waiters swished about between the gold-encrusted pillars.

'So your childhood was good?' Jean-Luc deduced as they ate.

'Yes, I was very happy.'

His smile was admiring, eyes glinting. 'I can imagine you being the adored daughter of an indulgent father!'

'Yes, he spoilt me dreadfully. Beautiful ballgowns, a vast allowance, extravagant parties.'

'Are you in close touch with your family? Planning to go back?'

Her face shuttered. 'No. I rarely contact them, except at Christmas, and I don't think I'll go back for some time.'

'Interesting.' He watched her, a glass of exceptional claret in one strong hand, his eyes narrowed.

'Why is that interesting?' she demanded, smiling tightly.

'Well,' he said deeply, frowning, 'it means that whatever Anthony did to you is somehow mixed up with your family.'

She put her knife and fork down with a clatter. 'I don't see how you can justify that very insolent and impertinent conclusion!'

'Simple.' The dark eyes watched her with an expression so close to deep personal pain that she was breathless with emotion until she heard his next words. 'It sounds as though he humiliated you in front of your friends, your family, the whole town, and you ran away to Paris because you couldn't face the ——'

'I'm not staying here listening to this,' she broke out rawly, getting to her feet. 'Thank you for dinner, *monsieur*, but I'm afraid I really must leave.'

'Sit down.' He leapt to his feet, his hand biting into her wrist. 'I brought you here to discuss this, and discuss it you will!'

'No!' She tried to get away from him, heart twisting in pain. 'I'm not putting up with this! I'm leaving!'

'All right, we'll both leave,' he said under his breath,

'but sit down while I get the bill and stop causing a scene! Do you have any idea where we are?'

'I don't care!' Tears were stinging her eyes; she wanted to crawl into a corner and die. 'Let me go, or I'll cause the biggest scene——'

'Is something wrong with the food, sir?' The *maître d'* arrived.

Jean-Luc flashed angry eyes at him. '*L'addition, s'il vous plaît!*'

'But sir, I——'

'*L'addition!*' he bit out, and the man scurried off.

Isabelle struggled angrily, trying to get away, but he held her wrist in merciless fingers, and with each struggle they tightened until she winced in pain. Meanwhile, their eyes warred, hers filled with bitter pain, his filled with hard determination.

'*L'addition, Monsieur Ferrat!*'

He tossed a platinum Am-Ex card on the plate, signed the slip in bold black handwriting, and never let go of Isabelle's wrist once. Seconds later, they left the hotel while people stared at Jean-Luc in recognition.

On the steps, a flashbulb exploded in the hot night.

'That's all I need,' Jean-Luc bit out under his breath, then raised a strong hand, beckoning the chauffeur, who slid up to the steps in the white Rolls-Royce convertible.

'I don't want to go home!' Isabelle said in alarm.

'I bet you don't!' He strode down the steps.

Panic rushed through her. 'Please. . .'

He studied her, unsmiling. 'I don't want you to cause another scene like that one. I won't have my personal life splashed all over the Press and I won't have *anyone* witnessing a row like that. Not ever. Do you understand me? It is never to happen again.'

'Of course. It won't happen again. I promise.'

'Good,' he said thickly. 'But I'm still not going to let you get away with it.' He put her in the back seat of the Rolls and slid in beside her, saying tersely to the chauffeur, '*Chez moi, plus vite.*'

The car shot away, and Isabelle looked frantically around for a route of escape, but within minutes they were pulling up outside the apartment.

'What are you going to do?' she demanded fiercely as he strode into the apartment building with her.

'Make you tell me what I want to know.' He stepped into the lift.

'You can't make me tell you!' she said fiercely, backing away from him as the lift rode up to the penthouse floor. 'And it's none of your business; it's not your place to know about my past!'

'If anybody gets taught their place tonight, it's going to be you.' The lift doors slid open and he caught her wrist, striding out.

'I'll scream if you lay a finger on me!'

'I'm aware of that.' He laughed under his breath. 'And I find the thought of it intolerably exciting.' He opened the door, whirled her through and strode to the bedroom corridor.

Panicking, she started to fight in deadly earnest. Jean-Luc opened his bedroom door, punched on the light and pulled her inside, slamming the door behind him. The silence prickled with sexual tension. Isabelle backed towards the double bed, heart slamming, eyes darting around the expensively furnished, dark and masculine bedroom.

'So. . .do you want to start talking now? Or making love?'

'Neither. . .' Her breathing was erratic. 'You can't do this. . .'

'Oh, I think I'll get away with it!' he said under his breath, and as he strode towards her the light glowed behind his dark head and Isablle felt a sexual excitement so strong it nearly made her fall to her knees.

CHAPTER FOUR

JEAN-LUC reached for her and she struggled not to let him sweep her into that dangerous desire, crying out angrily, pushing at his shoulders, fighting him, but he was too strong for her, too determined, and so was the excitement she felt, the clawing ache inside her to let him do anything he wanted with her, anything at all so long as it was physical. . .so long as it appeased the towering urgency that he had triggered since she first set eyes on his handsome face and powerful, sexy body.

'Don't touch me!'

He held her hard against him, his voice rough. 'Tell me what I want to know!'

'Go to hell!'

'Tell me!'

'No!'

'All right, then.' His eyes blazed with desire as he bent his dark head. 'Until you answer my questions — this is what you get!'

The hot onslaught of his kiss made her catch her breath, dizziness sweeping over her as her head tilted back, fingers clutching his broad shoulders, mouth opening passionately beneath his as she heard herself give a long, hoarse gasp of intolerable pleasure.

She kept struggling, though, little moans of excitement in her throat as her heart beat violently and her body brushed back and forth in exciting struggle against his until finally, finally, the darkness of their deep, private world opened up like a rush of hot black pleasure and overpowered the last protests in her mind.

And suddenly she was clinging to him, gasping with hot desire. The kiss was so necessary, so intense — they ravaged each other in the centre of the room, his hands moving up and down her body, rough sounds of excitement coming from the back of his throat at her towering response.

'*Mon Dieu!*' he bit out thickly, drawing a ragged breath, then swept her into his arms and carried her fast to the bed.

Kissing her back into the pillows, he spread her body expertly beneath his, one hard thigh parting hers while his mouth kissed her and his strong hands stroked her breasts and the hardness of his body burned into her.

His hand was on the zip of her black dress. It slid down, the gown falling softly away from her torso, and as her bare breasts bounced free his strong hands cupped them, stroking the nipples and inciting the cry of agonised desire from Isabelle that he knew would come.

Her body arched, filling his hands with her full, aching breasts. Her skin was prickling with intolerable excitement. She was blind with it, breathing hoarsely, the feel of his strong hands on her naked skin making her blood hiss like hot mercury about to explode. . .the first time any man had touched her naked skin for so long, so long. . .and then her mind exploded with the drive for him, his flesh.

I can't stand it any more, she thought frantically, and then her hands were fumbling with the buttons of his shirt.

He was darkly flushed, struggling out of his jacket, tearing his tie off in feverish haste so that she could get at his body, cufflinks clattering to the floor. Isabelle blindly pushed his shirt off with a gasp of tortured frustration and hunger—then she was touching him, feeling the violent thud of his heartbeat beneath that muscular, hair-roughened flesh.

'*Chérie. . .*!' he groaned thickly. '*Caresse moi. . .*'

Isabelle's hands moved everywhere with shaking passion, over his wrists, his black-haired forearms, his biceps, the hard shoulders, the firm muscled chest and down to the flat stomach, round to his spine, inciting shivers of excitement in Jean-Luc as he drew in his breath hoarsely, eyes closed hard, shuddering in delicious pleasure.

Their mouths met and clung. He stroked her thighs, kissing her, sliding long fingers over the silky flesh of her inner thighs as she writhed softly, passionately beneath him, delirious, her eyes closed, her mouth hot and hungry.

'*Ton corps me tourmente*!' He sounded feverish. '*J'ai besoin de toi, chérie*! I need you. . .'

She barely heard him, insensible now, blood boiling in her veins as her breath mingled hotly with his in their deep, passionate kiss, and all she could think was, I need this, I need *him*; he's the only man who's ever made me feel this way. . .

'*Je te veux*!' His fingers began sliding the dress down from her waist, his voice shaking. '*Ah, oui. . .je te veux*; I want you!'

'*Non. . .*' her swollen mouth whispered against his kiss. '*Non*!'

'Let me love you!' He was breathing raggedly, his heart slamming. 'Let me end this intolerable frustration for you, *chérie. . .*'

'No!' she said in sudden panic and self-hatred, grabbing his wrists as he slid the dress over her hips, her eyes flaring open with hot, dazed fear as she realised how much danger she was in. 'I said no!'

'Isabelle, it's what you need.' His voice was deep and husky and shaking. 'Let me give it to you.'

'You said you'd let me go if I agreed to talk!' she said desperately.

'I no longer want to listen.' His heart was banging loud and fast, his body rigid with excitement against her. 'All I want right now is to hear you crying yes, yes, yes as I make love to you!'

'That's something you'll never hear as long as you live!' Her voice shook with sudden appalled realisation of how close she had come to losing complete control. 'And don't think I don't know the real reason for your sudden fascination with me! You gave yourself away just now! You gave yourself away, Jean-Luc!'

He tensed, his face darkly flushed as he stared down at her.

'I don't know what I said in my sleep last night,' Isabelle whispered as tears stung her eyes, 'but it's despicable of you to try to take advantage of it! I may be celibate, I may be frustrated, and I may have given you the wrong impression just now, but that doesn't mean I'm going to give you anything else.' Her mouth shook. 'I won't let you take me!'

'Then why did you let it go so far?' He drew a hoarse breath.

'I'm human! I occasionally find myself giving in to temptation!'

'Occasionally?' His voice deepened as he struggled to control his fierce breathing. 'What do you mean? Have there been other men who got this response from you? You've done this before, taken it this far and——'

'No!' she said furiously. 'I've never behaved like this

with a man, never. And I hate you for making me do it. I hate myself, too, because I know the kind of man you are and I know you're just using me!' Bitter tears pricked her eyes. 'You make love to women and then just throw them away! Well, you're not doing that to me. No man is.'

'That's a reputation I gained in my twenties, Isabelle,' he said deeply. 'I'm thirty-six now. People change.'

She laughed angrily. 'Oh, don't try to tell me you've changed! Ever since I got here you've done nothing but try to get me into bed!'

'Has it ever occurred to you that I find you as exceptional as you obviously find me?'

Her green eyes stared intently for a split-second as she realised that that would be a miracle. It would change her life forever. It would make the bad days disappear and the golden, vibrant excitement of life rush over her again like magic dust. The dream flashed back into her mind, the locked chest containing her beautiful, confident self — and Jean-Luc saying deeply, with tenderness and understanding, 'I'll open it for you. . .'

But then she realised he was just flattering her, pandering to her fragile, shattered ego, and she despised herself for wanting to believe a man as wonderful as Jean-Luc Ferrat could possibly find her anything other than mildly amusing.

'Get off me!' she said, pushing at his shoulders.

'*Chérie*, I want to help you —'

'No, you don't,' she cut in thickly. 'I know what you really want, and you're not getting it!'

His mouth tightened. 'I could have taken you just now. I could still take you. Doesn't that tell you anything about me? Or about my real interest in you?'

'It tells me you're very clever!' she snapped, hating him. 'And before you try to kid me that you're not the man I know you to be, let me remind you of some very important evidence!'

'We're not in a court of law!'

'Look — you live here in Monte-Carlo exactly as a man of your reputation is supposed to. Fast sports cars, helicopters, and stunning blondes hiding in every corner just waiting for a kiss from you! It's perfectly clear that you're —— '

'I life my lifestyle,' he cut in. 'What's wrong with it? I like driving a Ferrari, living an international life and having women stare at me wherever I go. I also enjoy the respect and attention I get. Why shouldn't I? It makes me feel good to know I'm considered so desirable!'

'Oh, you conceited swine. . .!' She was breathless with shock.

'I am not conceited. I just have a very healthy self-assurance!'

'That's conceit,' she said uncertainly.

'It's self-assurance, Isabelle, and you obviously don't have it or you wouldn't be so convinced I only want to use you!' His dark eyes watched her in shrewd specu-lation. 'You're a very desirable creature yourself. Why do you have so little self-confidence when it comes to men? How can you believe I'm just amusing myself with you, when I'm quite obviously going crazy with unprecedented desire and can't keep my hands off you?'

She just stared at him, her heart banging, green eyes darting around nervously, afraid to consider the truth of what he'd said.

'Now come on.' He slid to one side of her body, breathing unsteadily, his hand on her bare stomach, watching her in the dimly lit bedroom. 'I want you to talk, and I very much want to listen. Tell me what has happened to make you like this.'

'No.' It was difficult to speak. 'I — don't want to tell you — '

'You will tell me, Isabelle, or I will make love to you immediately. No holds barred. No get-out clauses. I'm giving you this chance to talk instead of make love, but you won't get a second one. You may be used to living with frustration, but I'm not!' He watched her, his eyes intense and burning with emotion. 'Who was this man? Who was he and — ?'

'My husband.' Her eyes closed as she said the words. 'Anthony was my husband.'

There was a brief, tense silence. Jean-Luc stared down at her, the colour draining from his hard, handsome face. For a second he was just rigid with shock, his mouth a hard white line.

'Your husband?' he asked with hoarse disbelief. 'Your husband did this to you? But aren't you a widow? I mean — isn't he — ?'

'Yes, he was killed three years ago. He took the corner too fast on Lafayette Street, and drove straight into an office. He was drunk. And he was dead in fifteen seconds.'

Jean-Luc nodded slowly, staring. 'OK. . .' He expelled his breath, ran a hand through his dark hair. 'So he's been dead for three years. How long were you married to him?'

'A year.' She felt a tear slide out over her hot lashes and roll down her cheek, bitterly resenting having to tell him any of this because she knew he would think less of her, just as everyone else had.

'And what did he do that smashed your confidence to smithereens?'

'He. . .' She took a deep, shaky breath. 'He. . .married me because I was the most eligible girl in town.'

A hard smile touched his mouth, his dark eyes softening.

'I was a beauty queen,' she said softly, and flicked him a hurt little smile from under her long lashes. 'Was. Past tense. Miss New Orleans, the golden girl, they called me. My picture was in every shop window in town, every newspaper in town. . .'

He listened, smiling.

'And of course Anthony was the golden boy,' she went on, her smile fading into pain. 'Everyone said we were the perfect couple. He asked me to marry him after we'd been dating for a month.'

'How old were you when you married him?' he asked deeply.

'Twenty-two. I'm twenty-six now.'

'And how quickly did the marriage disintegrate?'

'Within a month.' Her voice grew raw. 'I found out he had two regular mistresses in New Orleans, kept in great luxury. He also frequently made casual pick-ups in both New Orleans and Baton Rouge.'

'What did you do when you found out about these other women?'

'I confronted him,' she breathed angrily, closing her eyes. 'And he said. . .he said——' She broke off, agony making her put her hands over her face.

Jean-Luc waited, then touched her cheek. 'Say it fast, be brief and try not to get emotional.'

Isabelle swallowed, then whispered, 'He laughed at me! He said I was hopeless in bed, had no idea what to do, and couldn't satisfy any man—least of all him!'

He gave a harsh sigh. 'And you were naïve enough to believe that he was right?'

'Of course he was right!' she said hoarsely. 'I was a virgin when I married him, and I didn't know what to do. I just felt so shy on my wedding night, and I — I made a mess of everything. I couldn't blame him for going with those other women. I was so inadequate as a lover that ——'

'Isabelle, don't say that,' he said deeply. 'It isn't true.'

'Don't you think I know that you're only trying to make me feel better!'

'Of course I'm trying to make you feel better. You're a beautiful woman who's had her confidence absolutely shattered. But if you're so inadequate, tell me, what am I doing lying in bed with you after you very sexily pushed half my clothes off?' His smile teased her. 'Hmm?' One long-fingered hand played with her red-gold hair. 'And why am I still here, doing everything possible to make sure I do one day make love to you properly?'

Her face flamed. 'I'll never let that happen! Never!'

'OK,' he said softly. 'We'll come back to that later. When did you realise your marriage was a nightmare?'

The question diverted her, and her lashes flickered as she confessed huskily, 'Not until he died. I went into shock when they told me about the crash. Just walked around like a zombie, thinking my life was over. Then, one afternoon, I was sitting in the garden of my parents' house and I saw a little girl with red hair running around, laughing, in the house next door. I —— ' She blushed, tears stinging her eyes. 'I know this sounds stupid, but I suddenly remembered myself, and how happy I was as a little girl, believing I was beautiful, that everyone loved me, and that I'd grow up to marry a handsome prince.'

'Ah, *chérie*. . .' He watched her with those dark

eyes, pain in their depths, a frown of compassion pulling his brows together.

'That's when I knew my marriage had been a nightmare.' Another tear slid over her cheek. 'And that's when I cried, for the first time since Anthony's death. I was ruined by then, you see. In the town ——'

'Everyone knew about Anthony's casual affairs?'

'Oh, he made sure they all knew!' she said bitterly. 'And he told them all that it was because I couldn't satisfy him. I was the town joke. Miss New Orleans, the golden girl who couldn't even satisfy her own husband.'

'Did you try to tell anyone the truth? That he was the one with the sexual problem?'

'He. . .?' She stared, then said unsteadily, 'But he was a brilliant lover, he must have been — all those women. . .'

'I think we can safely say he was a sexual cripple who conned his partners and abused his very beautiful and charming wife.'

She flinched, almost afraid to believe anything in that statement.

'Hmm.' He kissed her gently, then studied her. 'OK. . .so he died — and then you decided to go to Paris.'

Isabelle nodded. 'Yes, I. . . I knew I couldn't live any more as that woman — a failure in every area. So I just sold everything I had to get the plane fare, get to Paris, and get a flat within days so I didn't have to go crawling back with yet another failure in a long list of failures.'

'Very wise.'

Her eyes darted to his. 'I never regretted it. From the minute I arrived in Paris I felt as though a ten-ton weight had been lifted off my shoulders.'

'Which it had.'

'I got a job as a personal assistant immediately — my fluent French, of course, and my American secretarial training. But I kept to myself for the first year, never went out, didn't establish any kind of reputation other than one of quiet dignity. I just ignored every man I met, too.'

A smile touched the hard mouth. 'I'm sure there are a lot of very disappointed men in Paris.'

'The last thing I wanted was a man,' she said tightly.

'But that began to change,' he said deeply, 'didn't it? I imagine it took around two years for you to feel safe enough to start listening to the demands of your body.'

Her face ran with angry colour. 'I'm not even going to discuss that with you.'

'You are,' he murmured, 'or I'm going to start attending to them!'

Her heart raced and she said thickly, 'That's your answer to everything, isn't it? You really are a sex-crazed——'

'It's the only answer for you, *chérie*,' he said coolly, arching black brows. 'You must see that. Making love freely, hungrily and without restraint is the only way you'll be able to complete your recovery.'

'How very convenient for you!' she snapped, hating him.

He laughed under his breath. 'Yes, it is, isn't it? Very exciting, too. Three years' pent-up frustration. . . I can hardly wait!'

'And that's the only reason you're so interested in me, isn't it?' Her voice shook with fury.

'I'm interested in you,' he murmured, face darkly serious, 'because you are without doubt the sexiest woman I've ever met, and I have met a great many of the world's sexiest women!'

For a second the compliment rendered her breathless. Then she felt a fool for believing him even for one second. 'You're just saying that to try to make me feel better. But I know your motives! You think I'll be so grateful that I'll fall into bed with you.' Her eyes blazed. 'Well, you can take your compliments and stick them in the exhaust pipe of your bloody Ferrari, because I don't want them!'

He laughed. 'What a very inventive mind you have. Almost as fascinating as your unbelievably sexy body. And that, believe me, is really quite intoxicatingly sexy.'

Her eyes glittered like savage emeralds. 'You're very clever, *monsieur*! But I know what you really want from me!'

He laughed under his breath. 'I bet you do!'

Isabelle looked away, desire raging through her with terrible force, her heart banging as his long fingers slid over her breast and down to her slim hips.

'*Chérie*,' he said softly, stroking her thigh, 'we both know that you will eventually surrender and take what you need.'

'No!' She dashed his hand away. 'I'm not going to make the same mistake all over again by getting involved with a man who is just like my late husband!'

'Don't you compare me with that little creep,' he bit out through his teeth, that whiplash authority making her breathless. 'I've never abused a woman in my life! Or lied to one! Or destroyed one in order to hide like a desperate man from my own inadequacies! I don't need to! He obviously did, but that's not my fault, although it does appear to be rapidly becoming my problem!'

She was tense, recognising the truth of what he'd said about Anthony. It was what she had secretly thought for a long time.

'He damaged you badly,' Jean-Luc said curtly. 'But the damage was not irreparable. Everything you've done since his death has been done with courage and dignity. You've controlled your own recovery very skilfully, all the way down the line since his death.'

She felt her eyes prick with tears and blinked them back.

'However, the final hurdle demands that you lose control.'

Her eyes darted to his face.

'Lose it with me,' he said thickly.

'So you can reap the harvest of my frustration?' Her voice was low and shaking. 'I'd rather see you burn in hell!'

'I think, *chérie*,' he said deeply, 'that you would rather see me naked.'

Her eyes flashed over his powerfully muscled chest down to the black trousers, the long muscular legs splayed as he lay beside her, and she felt a desire so urgent that she almost had to bite her knuckles.

'The feeling is mutual.' His voice thickened suddenly, that smile fading as his eyes darkened. Then he slowly slid his strong hand to her breast, stroking her nipple to erect obedience as his thigh slid once again between hers, making her give a shaky moan of pleasure as his hot mouth buried itself in her naked, shivering throat.

Suddenly, laughter and shrieking voices came from the corridor.

He frowned, dark head lifting, face flushed. 'What the hell——?'

'Put the music on, Marie-Claire!' a voice called.

'James Brown, get on down!' Another voice.

Marie-Claire's high pitched giggle. 'Let's raid my

brother's drinks cabinet! He's always well-stocked with champagne!'

'That's all we need!' Jean-Luc bit out under his breath. 'Marie-Claire and her band of merry men, back from Jimmy'z!' He glanced at the Rolex on his dark-haired wrist. 'Midnight! I didn't expect her home till at least two a.m.'

Disappointment flooded over Isabelle so violently that she could barely speak. 'I suppose we'd better get up. . .'

'I don't think so, *chérie*!' He slid off the bed, striding like a magnificent animal across the room in those black trousers, muscles rippling in his tanned, tawny back. 'I'll lock the door and——'

But the door opened before he reached it.

'Oh, you are in!' Marie-Claire stopped in the doorway. 'I'm sorry, I thought——'

He tried to shut the door on her, but it was too late—she was already staring in shock at Isabelle clumsily dragging the duvet up to cover her bare breasts.

'Oh!' Marie-Claire was breathless, speechless, eyes darting.

'Don't ever come into my bedroom without knocking again!' Jean-Luc said under his breath. 'Look what you've done!'

'I'm sorry!' she whispered, staring up at him.

'Don't be sorry, just get out!' he said bitingly, and she stumbled backwards as he shut the door with an angry slam.

Isabelle was mortified, dragging her dress up, saying hoarsely, 'Oh, my God. . .oh, no. . .!'

He strode back to the bed rapidly. 'She had to find out some time. It must be fate that she found out now.'

'How can you be so calm? How can you put it down to fate?'

'Because I cannot change it.' He knelt on the bed on one knee, his hands deftly zipping her dress up. 'We'll have to get dressed and go and join them, though.' He was pulling his white shirt on, buttoning it, finding his cufflinks and threading them at his hair-roughened wrists.

Isabelle watched him through her lashes admiringly.

'It's one thing for her to know what's happened between us——' he shrugged on his black waistcoat, buttoning it swiftly ' — and another for us to flaunt it by staying in bed.' He bent to pick up his black jacket, shrugged it on, then stopped, frowning, looking around. 'What have you done with my tie, *chérie*?'

Hot colour scalded her face. 'Oh, I don't remember. . .' She fumbled about on the bed for a few seconds, then found it and held it out to him.

He took it, dark eyes rakishly amused, and slid it quickly round his strong neck, long fingers knotting it dextrously, then turned to her. 'So. We both look formal and dignified. Don't let her see that you are embarrassed or it will all be much worse.'

Isabelle got off the bed, slipped her high black shoes on, and walked with him to the door. Music came from the salon along the corridor. Low, gentle music and hushed voices.

'Oh, no!' Isabelle whispered. 'They're being so quiet now! She must have told them she found us together!'

'Marie-Claire would not dream of telling anyone what she has seen.'

'Then why are they so quiet?'

'Because they know that I am at home,' he drawled with a sardonic smile. 'And as I told you, *chérie*, I command a great deal of respect. I do it intentionally.

One can so easily control one's public image.' He opened the door to the salon, striding in beside her, his face suddenly changing, becoming hard and unsmiling, his eyes gleaming with dark power

Silence fell in the room. A large group of people stood huddled together by the balcony, and they all stopped talking as Jean-Luc Ferrat strode in, their faces reflecting absolute respect.

'Good evening,' Jean-Luc said coolly. 'Mademoiselle Montranix and I would love a glass of my champagne.'

A confused babble broke out as they all rushed to do his bidding.

'They're all terrified of you!' Isabelle murmured, glancing up at his strong face.

'Only because I make them so.' He bent his dark head and kissed her cheek. 'Had I invited them personally tonight, I would have greeted them with a smile and it would all have been different. We all have so many different personae, do we not?'

Her lashes flickered.

'Hmm.' A smile touched his hard mouth. 'Enjoy the party, *chérie*, but go to bed soon and sleep. You'll need all your energy tomorrow.'

'What for?' she said, startled.

'For me, *chérie*,' he drawled sardonically. 'I'm going to give you back your sexual confidence, and I can't tell you how much I'm looking forward to it!' He moved away, leaving her breathless with rage and fearful excitement.

Why did I tell him all that? she thought furiously. Why was I such a fool? Of course he'll take advantage of it — he's that kind of man, the arrogant swine!

Well, if he thinks I'm going to let him take me to bed he's got another think coming!

CHAPTER FIVE

NEXT day, Isabelle woke up feeling that her life had changed in some deep and complex way. The bedroom looked different to her, her skin felt renewed, even the sounds of Monte-Carlo outside her balcony windows seemed to be brighter, more vibrant, more exciting.

She remembered her conversation in bed with Jean-Luc, and her heart somersaulted with a combination of love and desire. He had seemed to understand so well. Sometimes there had been an expression in his eyes of mutual pain, as though something similar had happened to him. But how could it have done? A man like that, with so many women, such a world-famous reputation as a great lover. . . And the way he kissed, caressed, made love to her only convinced her that he was more than sure of himself where lovemaking was concerned. The memory of his hard body against hers was enough to make heat flood her skin, feeling again the touch of his hands and the throbbing pressure of his manhood against her thigh. . .she suddenly remembered what he had said. 'Why am I still here, doing everything possible to make sure I do one day make love to you properly?' Her love and desire disappeared instantly. How much clearer could he make it? He had probed into her painful past for one reason only: sex.

Isabelle got up, angrily determined not to let him get the better of her in any way, shape or form. She went to the bathroom, took a shower, and then went to the salon to find her friend.

'Hi. . .' Marie-Claire was on the balcony, watching her with guilty eyes. 'I'm so sorry about last ——'

'Don't apologise,' Isabelle said huskily, her face running with red colour. 'It wasn't your fault, and besides, my only real concern is that you shouldn't be upset by what you saw.' Sinking down on to the chair opposite, she watched her with anxious eyes. 'I'm here as *your* friend, after all, and it must have been awful for you to find me in ——'

'Oh, no, Isabelle!' Marie-Claire gave a stunned smile. 'I'm absolutely thrilled that you and Jean-Luc have got together!'

She stirred her café crème, frowning. 'Really?'

'Yes, I knew he'd be interested in you. You're a lethal cocktail of everything he most admires in a woman.'

Isabelle dropped her spoon, muttering, 'Oh, sorry. . .!'

'Anything wrong?' Marie-Claire watched her dive to retrieve it and bang her head on the table as she tried to sit up too fast, flustered.

'Nothing, no.' She felt breathless. 'I. . .where is he, by the way?'

'At work, of course. Which reminds me — he said to tell you lunch is confirmed.'

Her heart skipped rapid beats. 'Oh. . .?'

'Yes, he says you're to arrive at one. And tell the desk clerk your name. Then someone will be sent to take you to him.'

Isabelle felt like a sacrifice. Anger raced through her. What made Jean-Luc think she would even turn up for this lunch? He hadn't even asked her if she wanted to go, let alone if she was free.

'I don't think I'll go,' she said, her mouth tight.

Marie-Claire caught her breath, staring. 'What. . .?

But you can't be serious! He won't be pleased, Isabelle. He rarely meets people for lunch — he hates anything interfering with his work life. Besides. . . I thought everything was going so well between you!'

She forced a brief smile. 'I was just kidding. One o'clock, you say? Yes, I'll be there to meet him. In the meantime — what shall we do with our morning?'

Marie-Claire relaxed. 'We could go to the Oceanographic Museum. It's very beautiful, and right in the heart of Monaco town. . .'

Isabelle listened with half an ear, her gaze flickering over her friend's face. What did Jean-Luc have planned for her at lunchtime? He surely couldn't try to seduce her at work!

Later, she and Marie-Claire took a long, leisurely walk in the hot sunshine along the harbour, past the glittering yachts with the rock of Monaco rising beyond it. Then they went up the steep cobbled cliff path to the Oceanographic Museum, the streets of the old medieval town so steep that they were out of breath by the time they arrived.

'It was founded by Albert I in 1910,' Marie-Claire said as they got their tickets and wandered around the Oceanographic Museum. 'He was our scientific prince. He loved the sea and won international awards for his explorations and discoveries.'

The museum was impressive and amusing, complete with skeletons of peculiar-looking fish, some of them frighteningly big, and also a display of Jacques Cousteau's diving equipment, including his submarine. They completed their tour in the basement where the gigantic aquarium was illuminated blue-green, looking just like the deepest parts of the sea, while rare, weird and wonderful fish swam in the cool depths.

Walking back down into Monte-Carlo, they went

straight to the Hôtel Ferrat on the first section of the Avenue Princesse Grace.

'Here we are, then!' Marie-Claire said, standing at the foot of the white steps leading to the prestigious hotel with its gold-glass doors and liveried doorman. 'Jean-Luc's little home-from-home. The family business! Hôtel Ferrat!' She laughed, turning. '*A toute à l'heure!*'

Isabelle walked inside to find the hush of old money was redolent in the marble pillars, soaring domed ceiling, and the glittering chandeliers. A vast painting of Her Serene Highness Princess Grace hung on one wall, a portrait of Her Serene Highness Princess Caroline on another. The Monégasque flag of red and white was fluttering in the hot breeze outside the vast doors.

'Isabelle Montranix,' she said after walking across acres of marble to the desk clerk, 'to see Monsieur Jean-Luc Ferrat.'

The man's eyes widened. 'Please take a seat, Mademoiselle Montranix. I will telephone Monsieur Ferrat immediately.'

She moved away to a beautiful antique armchair by a marble pillar and sank down on it, seeing the wealthy, suntanned guests milling around the beautiful foyer. Were all Jean-Luc's hotels like this? It was so luxurious, and she suddenly had a glimpse of his background, a childhood of Monégasque style, wealth and social status. No wonder he was so sure of himself, so arrogant, so self-assured! Then she remembered that *Paris-Match* article about him, and how they had waxed lyrical about his business acumen, his ambition, and the drive that had taken him from being the heir to one fabulous hotel in Monaco, to one of the world's top hoteliers, all in just ten years. How could a man so

driven and admirable be such a swine when it came to
women? Surely he must have developed a little sensi-
tivity along the way? Of course not, she chided herself.
He was a womaniser with nothing but sex on his mind
where females are concerned. He had made that clear
enough last night.

'Mademoiselle Montranix?' A tall man in a dark
suit. 'Would you follow me, please? Monsieur Ferrat
is expecting you.'

She was taken across acres of expensive carpeting, up
in the chairman's lift, and across a vast floor of busy,
luxurious offices until they reached the boardroom.

'Please take a seat, Mademoiselle Montranix,' her
escort said as he opened the doors. 'Monsieur Ferrat
will be with you directly.'

She went into the vast, wood-panelled boardroom,
heard the door close behind her. A gigantic mahogany
table dominated the room. Two of the walls were
sheer windows, overlooking Monte-Carlo on one side
and the sea on the other.

It was one o'clock precisely. Isabelle sank down at
the head of the table and waited, her heart skipping
beats at the thought of seeing him again.

Suddenly, a door on the right opened and Jean-Luc
Ferrat strode in.

'*Ça va, chérie*?' he drawled coolly, formidable in an
impeccably cut light grey business suit, a watch-chain
glittering across a formal waistcoat, a rich silk tie
knotted at his throat and gold cufflinks gleaming at his
crisp white cuffs. 'You look lovely in that little dress.
Aren't you pleased to see me? Give me a kiss. . .'

As he bent his dark head, her pulses rocketed, his
mouth burning briefly over hers while she struggled
not to be so severely affected by the merest touch, the
merest kiss, the merest sign of his presence.

'Why did you invite me here like this?' she asked
tightly as he straightened from her. 'Without warning?'

'It was a decision I made overnight,' he drawled,
perching on the edge of the table in front of her, one
long leg bent. 'After our conversation in bed last
night. . .'

Her face ran with angry colour because she knew
that was exactly how she had remembered it this
morning, and she resented it. 'Kindly don't say it like
that! As though we're lovers!'

'Aren't we lovers, *chérie*?' he murmured with a
wicked smile. 'I'm sure I remember you tearing my
clothes off last night. . .'

'Look —— ' she was flustered ' — the truth is that we
hardly know each other, and you had no right to force
me into coming here today!'

'Nevertheless, you are here,' he drawled with a glint
in his dark eyes. 'And that is *my* chair you're sitting in!'

Her hands curved angrily over the arms of the vast
power-chair at the head of the table. 'I'll move, of
course!'

'No, you stay there.' He smiled sardonically. 'I like
to be above you. Have you eaten, by the way? I'm
afraid I find food rather mundane, but I can have
something brought up for you. The chef is excellent. I
stole him from a Paris hotel, and added a few extra
notches to my infamous reputation by doing so.' He
laughed. 'Most amusing!'

'I'm not hungry,' she said tightly, hating him.

'A drink, then?'

'No, thank you!'

He gave a cool smile and murmured, 'You're very
bad-tempered today. I can't wait to see how hard
you'll try to slap my face when you see the presents
I've bought for you. '

Her lashes flickered. She said slowly, 'Presents. . .?'

'Hmm.' His dark eyes glittered as he smiled lazily. 'I'll have them brought in, shall I?' He reached out a long hand for the telephone beside his strong thigh.

'Don't bother!' Her eyes flashed angrily. 'I don't want any presents from a man like you! You can't buy your way into my bed!'

'Kindly don't insult me,' he said icily, and the tone of his voice was stinging. 'Do I look the kind of man who has to buy his way into bed with beautiful women? What's the matter with you?'

'I didn't mean it like that. But you know I don't want you, and you seem determined to have me! What am I to think when you say you've bought me presents?'

'You're right,' he said flatly, eyes narrowing. 'I am determined to have you. But I must take into account everything you said last night. You have been badly damaged. Your sexual confidence is shattered. Your belief in yourself as a woman is practically non-existent.'

'Please stop saying it!' she burst out furiously, feeling humiliated. 'Can't you see that it just makes me feel worse?'

'Ah,' he said softly, smiling, 'but that is precisely where my presents come in handy.' He reached out one strong hand, picked up the telephone, punched a number. 'Ferrat. . .yes, bring them in.'

Isabelle watched him through her lashes. 'I shan't accept them, whatever they are!'

'Then I shall have them delivered to the apartment, *chérie*,' he murmured with a smile, 'as soon as you have refused them.'

There was a tap at the door, then it opened to his command, and two men strode in, each carrying a large square box which they placed on the table beside Jean-Luc and in front of Isabelle, before silently leaving the room again.

'Here.' Jean-Luc handed her one of the boxes. 'Open it.'

It was large and heavy. Isabelle unwrapped it curiously to see it was a white Chanel case, and as she flipped the gold lock it opened to reveal a dizzying array of products, all Chanel No.5.

'Oh. . .!' She stared, touched, then her eyes focused on the bottles of *huile de bain*, *huile pour le corps*, and she said tightly, 'What is this supposed to be for, *monsieur*?'

'To scent your skin,' he said softly, watching her. 'Bathe in Chanel bath oil, then perhaps a little scented dusting power from that pretty white pom-pom. . . I don't know, *chérie*. . .play with them as you please. . .'

Breathless, she stared up at him. '*Monsieur*, I don't think this is an appropriate present!'

'No? *Dommage*. I insist you accept it. And now. . .' he removed the white Chanel case from her lap, put it on the table and picked up the other gift box, handing it to her '. . .here is your second present.'

It was large and light. Isabelle tugged at the wrapping paper and it fell away to reveal a gold-embossed box from the world's most exclusive lingerie manufacturers.

'Oh, my God!' Isabelle gasped furiously. 'Lingerie? Oh! How dare you buy me lingerie?'

He laughed softly. 'Don't be angry. Here. . .' He tugged at the lid of the box. 'Open it. Don't you want to see what it looks like? Come on. . .open it and see, *chérie*, what I have chosen for you.'

'Get lost!' she said through tight lips, thrusting the

box at him. 'I've never been so insulted in all my life!'
She was on her feet. 'How dare you do this — how *dare*
you?'

'Sit down!' He was on his feet, one hand shooting
out to clamp over her wrist.

'No! You can't go out and buy me things like that! I
barely know you! I only met you ——'

'And you have already revealed more to me than to
any other man in your life! Last night you told me
your deepest secrets. Can you honestly say you feel
you don't know me?'

She couldn't reply.

'Now sit down, *chérie*,' he said deeply. 'I ceased to
be a stranger last night when I became your lover,
confessor and mentor.'

Isabelle felt her heart twist strangely with emotion,
her eyes lowering from his, unable to confirm or deny
what he had said, aware only that it was true, that
somehow he had forced it to be true, and that she
could not go back across the line of intimacy that they
had crossed.

She found herself sitting down, trembling, as he
released her with a long-fingered caress and sat down
on the edge of the desk too, watching her for a moment
in an intense silence.

Then he picked up the box and handed it to her.
'Your present, *chérie*. . .'

Isabelle stared angrily at it for a second, then
mutinously opened it, seeing the filmy tissue paper
inside and pushing it aside.

Her breath caught audibly as she saw the lovely,
lacy silk and satin items in colours which would perfectly match her skin and hair: ivory, pale pink, sky-
blue, cream and even black.

He watched her, smiling. 'I chose them myself. All

of them. As soon as the shop opened at ten o'clock this morning.'

'Well, you shouldn't have done!' she said thickly, still staring in veiled delight at the beautiful lingerie items.

'Ah, *cherie*,' he drawled slowly, 'I haven't bought lingerie for a beautiful woman in a long time.'

She looked up through her lashes, afraid to believe him. 'Don't pretend this isn't all just a game you've played a hundred times before, because I won't believe you!'

'I don't blame you,' he said coolly, arching dark brows. Then he gave a slow smile and slid long fingers across the silk, satin, lace items of lingerie, murmuring, 'But I enjoyed choosing them for you, *chérie*.'

Her pulses leapt with fearful arousal, but she said tightly, 'I hate them, and I won't accept them!'

'You may as well. If you give them back, what will I do with them?'

'Give them to your blonde?' she suggested angrily, stung.

'My blonde. . .?' He frowned, studying her.

'Forgotten her so soon?' Her voice thickened with savage jealousy. 'Very absent-minded of you, considering you were only kissing her last night in the foyer of the Hôtel de Paris!'

'Last night?' He stared. 'You saw us. . .? But why didn't you mention it?'

She lifted her head angrily. 'Because I don't care if you have ten million blondes, so long as you leave me alone!'

'*Chérie*,' he laughed softly, 'ten million? You exaggerate! But let me tell you about Louise Delavault. She is an old family friend, and you have no reason to be jealous of her!'

'Oh, please!' she said with an angry laugh. 'I'm not remotely jealous — and I also don't believe she's just your friend!'

He smiled slowly. 'At any rate. . . I insist you keep the beautiful things I bought for you. They will be delivered to the apartment by one of my men later this——'

'I told you, I don't want them!'

'Perhaps you'll feel differently if you go home and play with them for the afternoon.'

Her eyes flashed. 'I very much doubt it! In fact, if you have these things delivered to the apartment against my wishes I will throw them all in the nearest dustbin!'

'Do that,' he bit out under his breath, 'and you'll make me angrier than you've ever seen me! And you wouldn't like it if you made me that angry! You wouldn't like it at all!'

She felt intimidated, but refused to show it. 'I won't be browbeaten by you, *monsieur*! Or bullied into a seduction I have no intention of allowing to take place!' She paused, adding stiffly, 'However, I understand that you've gone to a great deal of trouble, and that it would be churlish of me to throw your gifts away.'

He smiled sardonically, tapping his foot.

Anger rushed through her. 'Don't think you just got the better of me, because I——'

'Shh!' He touched her cheek with a long hand. 'No more arguments. Now go home and wait for your presents to arrive. Think about the pleasure I got from choosing them for you.'

Her lashes flickered and she nodded jerkily.

'It would give me even more pleasure to see you

model them for me tonight when I get home from work.'

'You must be out of your mind,' she said through her teeth. 'I wouldn't even put one of those ridiculous garments on, let alone parade about in them for you!'

His strong hand slid suddenly on to her hot throat, felt the pulse beating wildly there. 'Oh, I think you might indulge me, *chérie*,' he murmured. 'Especially if you spend the afternoon thinking about it. And I want you to promise me you'll think of nothing else.'

'I shall throw them in the bottom of my wardrobe!'

'Take them out and feel them against your skin first.'

'No! I don't like any of this! I don't like what's happening between us ——'

'That's because you're fighting it. It's only natural to be afraid when you reach the final hurdle. Many of the world's greatest racehorses would balk, too. Particularly those that are highly strung and have been badly treated.'

Her green eyes darted to his strong face.

'You just need an experienced hand to guide you,' he murmured. 'Now go home, *chérie*, and think about what I have said. Look at the things I have bought you, and wait for me at seven in your bedroom.'

'I will go home, *monsieur*, but I will not look at the things you've bought me, and I will not be waiting in my bedroom for you at seven!'

Isabelle got to her feet and left the room without another word, shutting the door angrily behind her.

Furious, she took the lift down and strode through the luxurious marble foyer with hatred sparkling in her green eyes. How dared he do all this? She was absolutely incoherent with rage.

Hot sunlight blinded her as she went down the white

steps, the sea in front of her, the hot, sun-bleached streets filled with traffic. She wished she could burn all that lingerie right in front of him, the swine.

When she got home, she found that Marie-Claire was not there. The apartment was empty, but the balcony doors were still open and the room shone with fresh polish.

Madame Dusort was listening to the radio in the kitchen, singing along to a song while she baked fresh baguettes. '*En direct de Monte-Carlo. . .!*' the jingle announced as the song came to an end.

'*Ça va, madame!*' Isabelle said as she went into the kitchen. 'Did Marie-Claire tell you where she was going?'

'To the Country Club for a game of tennis,' Madame Dusort told her with a breezy smile. 'I expect she'll be out all afternoon.'

Isabelle nodded, made herself a long, cool fruit punch, then went out on to the balcony to stare out at Monte-Carlo and feel furious with Jean-Luc for his unbelievable insolence.

The doorbell rang twenty minutes later. Isabelle tensed angrily, aware that it was probably a delivery for her, and, sure enough, Madame Dusort called out, 'Delivery for you, *mademoiselle*! Where shall I put them?'

Her face flushed angrily as she said, 'My bedroom, please!'

She tried to stay out on the balcony and not be curious, but after fifteen minutes the lure of all that sensuality drew her to the bedroom, and very soon she was holding the beautiful lingerie up to her skin, feeling the silk, the satin, the lace. . .

He would not be home until seven. Her eyes drifted to the Chanel case. It was years since she had bathed in such hedonistic sensuality. She wanted to, suddenly, so much. . .

At three, she was languishing in a vast bath-tub filled with Chanel-scented *huile de bain*. When she emerged, she felt so wonderful that she just had to touch that vast white dusting puff, smiling as she lay nude on the vast double bed, toying with it, laughing softly as she tapped it on her nose and breathed in the soft scent, wrinkling her nose then rolling over, naked and softly dry, tapping the white puff over her body, playing for a while before her eyes drifted inevitably to the lingerie.

Oh, she so much wanted to try them all on. . .

Sliding naked and scented from the bed, she went to the antique table where the white gold-embossed box lay, and a second later was sliding into the pink silk teddy, gasping at its beauty as the fan whirred overhead and she felt the silk with her hands, turning this way and that in front of the mirror, thinking, Oh, he chose so well. . .

Singing softly to herself, she stood in front of the mirror, the pink silk teddy gleaming on her sun-kissed, scented skin, and held up other beautiful items of lingerie against herself, smiling. . .

There was a knock at the door.

Isabelle jumped, heart banging violently, and ran to the bed, grabbing her dressing-gown and hurriedly dragging it on, not wanting Madame Dusort to see what she was up to.

'Come in!' she called unsteadily, belting her robe.

The door opened.

Jean-Luc walked coolly inside and Isabelle gasped shakingly as she saw him, and felt his dark eyes race over her as he closed the door and leant on it, watching her through those heavy eyelids, unsmiling.

'Oh, God. . .!' She was breathless, heart thudding loudly. 'What are you doing here? It's only four o'clock! You said——'

'I changed my mind.'

'You did it deliberately! You knew I'd——'

'Be unable to resist.' He nodded, his face taut with desire. 'Oh, yes, I knew, *chérie*. And when I rang twenty minutes ago Madame Dusort told me you were in the bath. I drove home immediately.'

She was trembling.

'It's quite unprecedented——' his eyes were jet-black with desire '—for me to take time off work. So you see, *chérie*, how very much I want to know what you are wearing under that pretty little robe.'

Her heart was banging so loudly now that she thought she'd faint. 'I'm not wearing anything!'

He laughed unsteadily and walked towards her.

'No!' She backed away, shaking. 'Get away from me!'

He reached for her, pulling her against his hard body.

'No. . .!' She fought him breathlessly. 'Please. . .'

'Don't fight me,' he said under his breath, sitting her down on the bed beside him, his dark eyes moving to the open neck of her robe. 'Let me see, *chérie*! Let me see you. . .' He tugged at the belt.

'No!' Isabelle tried to grab it, but he took her wrists and pulled the robe apart to reveal the pink silk teddy.

He stared down at her body in the pink silk and drew a harsh breath. 'Yes. . .that was my favourite, too.'

'Oh, God. . .!' She trembled from head to foot, her skin rushing with heat, her eyes closed, arms spread wide.

'Take off the robe, *chérie*,' he said thickly.

'No!' Her body was throbbing with pulses.

'I don't want to remove it forcibly,' he said unsteadily. 'That would destroy the sensuality I have evoked. But I want to see you so much that I'm afraid I *will* remove it if you continue to refuse.'

'If I take off my robe, you'll see it as an invitation to make love to me, and I won't let you do that!'

'I'll certainly see it as an invitation to kiss you,' he said thickly, 'but I swear I will not touch you intimately unless you ask me to. You have my word, *chérie*. There will be no force between us.'

Isabelle remained still, one long, slender leg bent on the bed, one long, slender leg sliding off, foot almost touching the floor, and her robe open to reveal her beautiful body in the pink silk teddy.

Slowly, she lifted trembling fingers to slide the robe off. It dropped softly to the floor.

Jean-Luc drew in his breath slowly, shakingly, staring at her body as she trembled before him, her heart thudding with terrible excitement, her breath coming faster and faster and faster. . .

'You're beautiful!' He slid a strong hand to her waist, staring down at her body. 'Ah, Isabelle. . .!'

She looked at him hotly through her lashes, her lips moistened by her tongue-tip in unconscious invitation.

With a rough groan he pulled her into his arms, and his hot mouth came down over hers in a long, slow, sexy kiss that made her slide against him with a moan, helpless to fight the onslaught of sheer sensual desire that was flooding her veins as her arms went around his strong neck and her mouth opened beneath his.

Suddenly, he was sliding her full length on the bed, his mouth more demanding, his breathing ragged as he found her body sensual, scented, silk-clad and more than willing beneath his.

'Jean-Luc. . .' her swollen mouth murmured hotly against his, and her hands stroked his dark hair, her body arching up against his, needing physical contact from him, longing now to feel his hands on her body, allowing her slender, naked legs to part for him as he moved slowly against her, spreading her sensually beneath him and hearing her delirious gasps and moans of longing for his hands.

'You want me to touch you, *chérie*?' he asked thickly against her passionate, swollen mouth.

'Yes, yes. . .' She heard her slurred moan through the pounding of blood in her body, and a second later felt the firm hands move to caress her aching breasts through the thin silk.

His mouth was burning down over hers, his strong hands slowly, sensually baring her breasts, caressing them, sliding fingers strokingly over her skin, making her shiver and gasp and slide against him.

She was delirious, so aroused that she could only go with her body as it pulsed and rocked instinctively against his, and then she felt his hand slide caressingly over her spread thighs, moving upwards, upwards until she felt his palm warmly cover the pulsing apex of her body.

Her breathless cry was moving in its intensity as his hand touched her gently above the pink silk which hid the hot, moist flesh that no man had touched for three years.

He groaned suddenly, his voice hoarse with desire, and his fingers stroked the silk teddy from her shoulders, his heart banging hard as he kissed her, baring her slowly to the waist, breathing raggedly.

'Oh, Jean-Luc!' she whispered passionately, shivering with sensual pleasure as his long fingers moved to stroke the silky, scented skin of her inner thighs,

FOUR FREE

Temptations

TRUE LOVE
ELISE TITLE

NOT
MY BABY!
JUDITH McWILLIAMS

BEWITCHING
CARLA NEGGERS

WE

Plus!

a cuddly Teddy Bear and a Mystery Gift FREE

Mills & Boon Temptations bring you all the excitement, intrigue and emotion of modern love affairs.

And to introduce to you this powerful, highly charged series, we'll send you four Mills & Boon Temptations, a cuddly Teddy Bear PLUS a Mystery Gift, absolutely FREE when you complete and return this card.

We'll also reserve you a subscription to our Reader Service which means you'll enjoy:

- FOUR SUPERB TEMPTATIONS - sent direct to you every month.
- FREE POSTAGE AND PACKING - we pay all the extras.
- FREE MONTHLY NEWSLETTER - packed with competitions, author news and much more.
- SPECIAL OFFERS - exclusively for subscribers.

CLAIM YOUR FREE GIFTS OVERLEAF

FREE BOOKS CERTIFICATE

Yes! Please send me **Four FREE Temptations** together with my **FREE gifts.**

Please also reserve a Reader Service subscription for me. If I decide to subscribe, I shall receive four superb new titles for just £7.80 each month postage and packing FREE. If I decide not to subscribe I shall contact you within 10 days. Any free books and gifts will remain mine to keep. I understand that I am under no obligation whatsoever - I may cancel or suspend my subscription at any time simply by contacting you. I am over 18 years of age.

7A4T

Ms/Mrs/Miss/Mr _____

Address _____

_____

Postcode _____

Signature _____

MILLS & BOON READER SERVICE
FREEPOST
PO BOX 236
CROYDON
CR9 9EL

spread in melting invitation for him as his long fingers found the heat searing the damp silk.

'Ah, *je te veux*!' He drew a hoarse breath, dragging air into his lungs. 'I want you so much I'm practically on fire!'

He suddenly started tugging at his tie with shaking hands, face darkly flushed and eyes burning as he slid the tie off, threw his cufflinks to the floor, began to shoulder out of his jacket.

'What are you doing?' Isabelle felt herself coming out of that pulsing, sensual reverie, staring at him in horror. 'You said you wouldn't ——'

'You asked me to touch you!' he said hoarsely. 'You asked me to!' He expelled his breath in a ragged exclamation of intense excitement. 'Ah, Isabelle — let me take you. . .let me make love to you. . .!'

'No!' she whispered hoarsely, eyes wide with horror.

'Yes!' he said shakily, fire in his eyes, and his hot mouth claimed her again, kissing her deeply.

'No, I said no!' She started to fight him, blind with fear now, her hands hitting his broad shoulders and trying to claw at his face.

He jerked his head back. 'All right, all right!' His hands caught her wrists and pinned them to the bed, staring down at her with fury. 'I won't rape you; calm down!'

She gave a faint little sob, her mouth trembling as she stared up at him, heart banging with the realisation of just how far she had gone and just how quickly it had all got out of control, as it always did with Jean-Luc and probably always would, her desire for him now becoming dangerous.

'Why won't you let me make love to you,' he asked shakily, 'when you know as well as I do that I'm the only one who can give you everything you so badly need?'

'Because it isn't all I need!' She felt the sudden, unexpected prick of hot tears in her eyes. 'I need love, too!'

He watched her in silence for a moment, then his mouth curved sardonically. 'Ah, yes. . .*l'amour*! I wondered when you'd bring that particular subject up!'

Her mouth trembled. 'What's wrong with the subject of love?'

'Nothing. Except that I am not discussing it in bed with you.' He moved away from her, getting off the bed, raking a hand through his black hair and bending to pick up his cufflinks, his face cool. 'Get up, get dressed—we're going out.'

CHAPTER SIX

THE red Ferrari sped along the Boulevard Princesse-Charlotte, the warm breeze from the open sunroof lifting Jean-Luc's black hair from his tanned forehead as he surveyed the road with narrowed eyes behind a pair of dark glasses. Isabelle sat beside him, dressed now in a red sundress that enhanced the vivid red-gold of her hair.

'Where are we going?' she asked him tightly.

'Le Jardin Exotique,' he drawled. 'You haven't seen it, have you? No? Good—it's very beautiful. And besides. . .' a hard smile curved his mouth '. . .I had to get out of that bedroom, *chérie*, or I would have lost my self-control and taken you. It was a very close thing. You're lucky I'm not the swine you keep telling me I am.'

Her face flamed. 'Look, I didn't orchestrate that! You did, by buying those things and——'

'I know.' His hand slid to her thigh caressingly. 'And I'm delighted with your response. But I knew you would bring up the subject of love sooner or later, and it was always my intention to discuss it somewhere other than the bedroom.'

'Why?' she asked, hope burning like fire inside her as she thought, Does he love me? Could a man like this possibly ever——?

'Because, *chérie*——' his deep voice cut into her thoughts '—sex has very little to do with love. And I want to underline that to you.'

Her mouth whitened and she looked away, feeling

99

sick inside, pain tugging at her heart as she realised yet again what a fool he could make of her, and how easily she could fall in love with him if she once stopped fighting.

'You hardly need to underline that!' her angry, hurt voice said. 'You've made it more than clear that your only interest in women is sexual. Why should I be any different?'

'Why indeed?' he said oddly, a flash of emotion in his dark eyes.

The Ferrari roared up bright-lit streets, up slopes, past banks and shops and apartment blocks glittering in the sun, up towards the invisible border, until they arrived at Le Jardin Exotique.

Isabelle stepped out of the car and walked with Jean-Luc at her side into the garden, the sound of crickets chirping in the heat, the scent of hot earth, dusty rock and the sight of vivid flowering cacti from Mexico, South America and Africa all combining to make her think briefly of New Orleans and of Texas.

'This is just beautiful,' Isabelle remarked as they walked up the steep sun-baked paths. 'It reminds me of summers in Texas.'

'Texas?' His brows rose. 'Ah, yes. . .just next to Louisiana.'

'I have some cousins who live there. I used to visit them every vacation.' She studied the cacti. 'Texas is very close to Mexico, so I can understand why they have cacti there. But how is it possible for them to grow here like this?'

'Because of the cliff,' Jean-Luc told her. 'It has the ideal angle for receiving the hottest rays of the sun, and the slope just lets any rain or moisture drain off.'

'Ah. . .' She walked on, deeply aware of him, and

of the heat, the dry earth, the vivid flowers and the subject of love.

'So,' Jean-Luc murmured with a cool smile, 'you want to talk about love with me?'

Her heart skipped a beat. 'I said I wouldn't let you make love to me because I wanted more than just sex. I wanted love, too.'

'Are you telling me you're in love with me?'

She caught her breath and stopped walking, staring at him. 'Am I what. . .?'

'It's a perfectly simple question, *chérie*.' He stopped too, looking at her from behind those dark glasses. 'Are you in love with me?'

'No!' Her heart twisted with love even as she said it.

He studied her, towering there in his white shirt and dark waistcoat, hands in grey trouser pockets, Monte-Carlo in the distance far below, the sea shimmering in a heat-haze mist, tall bleached buildings beside tiny white boats in the far-off harbour.

'Let me see if I understand you correctly,' he murmured. 'You say you won't make love with me unless love is involved. Yes?'

'Yes. . .' she said slowly, lashes flickering in the heat.

'But you are not in love with me?'

'No.'

'So — who exactly is supposed to provide the necessary ingredient of love in this exchange?'

She stared at him, speechless. The heat was burning down on her head, her bare arms, shimmering on the red silk of her hair as it fell across her scarlet sundress.

'You want me to love you,' he drawled softly, his smile mocking, 'without love in return. Is that it?'

'No, I ——'

'*Chérie*, the world is a market-place, for better or

worse, and we all have to give something in order to get what we want.'

'Yes, but ——'

'You know that I want your body very badly — and you just told me exactly what you want in return for it.' His eyes narrowed, his smile suddenly hard. 'My heart on a platter!'

'Jean-Luc, I never said anything of the sort!'

'No,' he drawled expressionlessly, 'you didn't. So let us end this conversation for the moment.' He turned and started walking again.

Isabelle fell into step beside him, confused by the conversation, shooting occasional glances at his tough profile as they climbed higher on the cliff, the paths dry stone, the cacti growing in thick profusion now, vivid red colour blazing against the rocky white-stone cliffs, and Monte-Carlo getting smaller and smaller in the distance.

Why had he interpreted her words like that? The question sprang into her mind like a hothouse flower, forcing its way to the surface as the possible answer came shooting along like a bullet behind it. Was he in love with her?

She felt breathless, staring at his hard face as he walked beside her. Is he in love with me? she thought. It's not possible! But what if he is. . .? Oh, she felt utterly dazzled, knocked for six, feeling her own capacity for love springing forth, and within seconds she was flying up into fairy-tales, thinking, My life would be repaired forever! A man like Jean-Luc Ferrat, in love with me! It's a dream come true!

He stopped walking suddenly, glanced down at the view. 'Isn't Monaco beautiful from up here?'

'Yes. . .' She stared at his hard, handsome face.

'You like the gardens?' He turned back to look at

her, standing in front of her, hands thrust in grey
trouser pockets as the buttons on his waistcoat
gleamed in the sun and his shirt was dazzlingly white.

'I love them,' she said huskily, thinking, You're
wonderful, I could fall in love with you so easily, so
very easily. . .oh, God, and if you were in love with
me, what would the world say, what would the world
think?

'So tell me,' he drawled, 'just as a matter of interest.
What would you do if I were in love with you?'

She was so breathless that her head was spinning.
'Are you?'

'It's a theoretical question, *chérie*. I want a theoretical answer.'

'Oh. . . I don't know, Jean-Luc. What would I
do. . .? I'd be very flattered, thrilled even, and I'd
love you a little in return.'

He laughed softly, drawling, 'Would you? Well, I
think that's very nice. . .'

Alarm stirred in her for the first time and she felt
her smile begin to fade as she saw the trap too late.

'You little bitch!' he said under his breath, his smile
barbed. 'You'd be flattered and thrilled and love me a
little in return? A *little*?'

'Jean-Luc, I——'

'My God, you're dangerous!' he whispered, eyes
staring into hers, black with glittering, savage emotion.
'Underneath the hurt, frightened little girl who needs
my sexual skills there's Scarlett O'Hara, just waiting
to leap out and add my heart to her collection!'

Her face flamed. 'That's not true! Jean-Luc, I didn't
mean it like that!'

'Oh, you meant it all right!' he said thickly. 'And
why not? You're recovering fast, your sexual confi-

dence is blossoming, and now you want it all back, just the way it was before you married Anthony!'

'No. . .'

'Yes, Isabelle! And I know exactly who you were before you married that man! Miss New Orleans — remember? The golden girl, twisting Daddy round her little finger. Just one flash of those beautiful eyes and another man's heart went snap!'

'No, I wasn't like that. . .' Her voice tailed off in horror as she met his eyes and felt the hard power of his mind ram into her heart like an iron fist. I *was* like that, she thought. I was. . .

'And that's why you ran from New Orleans. Because when a golden girl is stripped of her magic she has nowhere to go but out, through the nearest exit, and never return until she is golden again.'

There was a brief, tense silence.

'Don't look so surprised, *chérie*,' Jean-Luc said under his breath. 'Did you really think I was a fool? Listening to your sad story without putting all the pieces together and seeing exactly who I was dealing with?'

She could barely breathe, barely speak; she felt staked stark naked to this damned white-hot cliff above Monaco.

'I read between the lines, *chérie*! You were treated badly by your late husband, but how heartlessly did you treat men before you married him?'

'I. . .' She struggled to speak, to be strong and honest, as he was being with her. 'I never meant to be like that, Jean-Luc! It just happened and I accepted it because I didn't know any other way to live.'

'But you broke plenty of hearts along the way.'

She stiffened, then nodded jerkily, lowering her gaze.

'Well, you're not breaking mine,' he said thickly.

Her head came up angrily. 'I never wanted to!'

'Never wanted to?' He stepped towards her, his smile dangerous. 'I bet you've been praying for it since the minute I started chasing you!'

'No! I never at any time thought——'

'What if Jean-Luc Ferrat should fall wildly in love with me?' he said fiercely, taking her shoulders. 'Oh, that would really repair all the damage done to your poor little beauty queen heart, wouldn't it?'

She winced, because that was exactly what she had thought as they walked up here.

'Hit a nerve, did I?' he bit out roughly. 'I'll hit more than a nerve if you ever try that particular skill on me, *chérie*! You're up against a lifetime award-winner! If anybody gets their heart broken around here, it's not going to be me!'

'Get away from me!' she said fiercely, struggling.

'Who the hell did you think you were playing with?' he bit out. 'I knew exactly who you were, the minute I saw you, standing there at Nice airport like a goddess, looking me up and down as though I ought to be on my knees!'

'I didn't look at you like that!'

'Oh, yes, you did, *chérie*, until I realised that what you wanted from me was exactly what you very nearly got this afternoon!'

'Shut up, you vicious swine!'

'Oh, I'm vicious, am I? You want to toy with my affections, make me fall in love with you, then run away back to New Orleans with the name "Jean-Luc Ferrat" stamped on your conquest list, to crow with delight over my personal despair? And I——' his voice was hoarse '—am vicious? I could nail your heart to my bedpost and God himself would call it justice!'

'All right!' She pushed at him, dashing his hands from her shoulders, head lifted and eyes blazing with angry honesty. 'It's true! I did think how it would be if you fell in love with me! You're a very famous, desirable man and I'd be a fool if I didn't consider the cachet I'd receive from having you fall for me!'

He gave a harsh laugh, but there was a spark of angry admiration in his dark eyes as he studied her.

'I'm human,' Isabelle said thickly. 'For a moment, I was tempted. But I didn't ever really think it was possible. How could I think it? Look at who you are — just look at yourself, Jean-Luc, and then look at me. It's absurd to even consider that —— '

'*Chérie*,' he cut in, arching black brows, 'I want to restore your confidence, not destroy it. Don't run yourself down just because I've cornered you and made you admit your own fatal flaws. You did consider breaking my heart. The idea thrilled you, of course — that is in your nature. I knew that all along. In New Orleans, you were once such a woman. A heartbreaker and a flirt. And that part of you will resurface as your confidence grows.'

Her eyes, dazzlingly green, flicked to his from beneath her lashes.

'But you will not cut your second set of Scarlett O'Hara teeth on me,' he said under his breath. 'And if you try to, Isabelle, I warn you, I will break your heart into tiny pieces and scatter it to the Mistral.'

She trembled against him, aware that he could do it, suddenly appalled by the realisation that she was already standing on the very edge of falling in love with him, her heart already spinning into his hands, leaving her breathless with respect, admiration. . . and love.

'*Tu as compris*?' he murmured, dark brows arching coolly.

She nodded, breathless, her bright head lifted to stare at him.

'Good.' He kissed the top of her head. 'In that case, I think our conversation is now over. We'll go home. . .'

They walked back down the cliff in tense silence. Isabelle felt almost more frightened now of his growing effect on her heart than she did of his overwhelming effect on her body. From the start, he had been dangerous to her, but it had seemed only a sexual danger. Now she felt love growing unstoppably and she was afraid.

The red Ferrari roared back through the hot, winding, glittering slope-streets, down into Monte-Carlo, and Isabelle watched his strong hand relaxing coolly on the console, remembering it stroking her breast this afternoon, understanding her body as easily as he understood her mind.

I'm going to fall in love with him.

The thought shot at her like a bullet out of a gun, then, hard on the heels of that, another bullet.

I'm already falling in love with him.

She felt fear rush over her skin, hot-cold like a state of shock. The road in front of them swam. She had never felt so frightened in her life, as though she was on a slippery slope, screaming and trying to climb back up, every effort in vain, every struggle useless, because she had nowhere left to go but down, into the dark reservoirs of love.

Jean-Luc zipped the Ferrari into the underground car park with one smooth turn, parked it next to the open-topped white Rolls-Royce, and switched off the engine.

'OK.' He locked the wheel with a cool turn of his hand. 'Let's go in and have a cool drink. It's five-thirty, and Marie-Claire will probably be home by now. We'll join her.'

They got out of the car. Suddenly Isabelle said, 'I don't want this to continue.'

He turned, halfway across the stone floor, frowning. 'You don't want what to continue?'

'This.' She was dry-mouthed, staring at him across the car park. 'Our involvement. I—I want to end it, Jean-Luc. Right now.'

His dark lashes flickered. Slowly, he walked towards her, stood in front of her, looking down into her pale, frightened face. 'It's too late, Isabelle,' he said deeply. 'It's gone too far and you're in it right up to your neck, just as I am.'

She stared with hope into his eyes. 'What do you mean. . .?'

Jean-Luc tensed, then gave a cool smile. 'Just that I've put in too much hard work, *chérie*, to let you get away from me now. I intend to make love to you. And you will remain in Monaco until I do.'

Pain ripped her heart like a lion's claws. 'I'm not waiting around to be seduced! I'm leaving Monaco today, and you can't stop me!'

'Oh, can't I? You set one foot outside this principality without my say-so, and I'll be right behind you with a team of detectives, ready to bring you back.'

She stared at him with incredulous rage. 'You can't do that!'

'I can and I will,' he said thickly, eyes hard. 'You should have left Monaco when you first realised what was going to happen between us. It's just too late, now, Isabelle. I won't let you get away from me. Not until I've got what I want from you.'

'You can't keep me here!'

'I can bring you back every time you try to leave.'

'I'll tell the authorities!'

'That's up to you. But the consequences will be just exactly what you're trying to run away from.' He bent his dark head, kissed her mouth burningly, his face flushed as he dragged his hot mouth from hers, then raked a hand through his hair and said thickly, 'Now, let's go and see Marie-Claire. We've neglected her for too long.'

They rode up in the lift together, and he lounged against the wall beside her, his body close, one hand toying with her red-gold hair, a passionately possessive smile on his tough mouth.

'*Ciao*, lovebirds!' Marie-Claire called out as they went into the salon.

'Hello, pest,' drawled Jean-luc. 'Win your match at the club?'

'No, lost two sets to one.' Marie-Claire lounged on the creamy couch in cut-off denims and a leopard-skin-print silk top, watching Michael Jackson on MTV. 'Why are you home early from work?'

'Isabelle and I went to Le Jardin Exotique for the afternoon.'

'What. . .?' Marie-Claire sat up, staring. 'You took the afternoon off *work* to go out with Isa——'

'Yes,' he cut in, face hard, eyes narrowing. 'And we decided, while we were out, that we'd been neglecting you. So I'm going to take you and all your friends out to dinner tonight. My treat. OK?'

Marie-Claire gaped at him. 'What—all of them?'

'A select handful,' he drawled wryly. 'Say seven or eight. Book a table for eight o'clock. Anywhere you like.' He turned on his heel. 'I'm going to take a quick shower. I'll see you both later.'

Isabelle watched him go, her heart twisting. Then she turned to Marie-Claire, conscious that she had patiently stepped aside in order that Jean-Luc could spend time with her.

'What's on MTV?' she asked brightly. 'Anything fun?'

'Oh, yes, my favourite group.' Marie-Claire laughed, turning the sound up as the all-girl group slid sensuously on to the screen in long, slit-to-the-thigh red dresses and started singing very sexily about giving their man something he could feel.

Isabelle sat with Marie-Claire, watching the screen, and thinking of Jean-Luc. He refused to allow her either to end the involvement or leave the apartment. What was she supposed to do? She couldn't let him pull her in deeper than she already was. That route would lead to disaster, because she knew she was very nearly in love with him, and she was so frightened of that, for many reasons, some of them to do with the past, but most of them to do with *his* past, and his cavalier attitude to women. He'll never love me, she thought, her skin going icy with fear. Never in a million years. And I *must* guard myself against him.

At seven, Marie-Claire went to take a brief shower and change. Isabelle went into her bedroom. She took her clothes off, wrapped a bath-towel around her, and stared unseeingly into the wardrobe. What was she going to wear? Her heart lurched with violent emotion at the thought of Jean-Luc. What does it matter what I wear? she thought in sick fear. He will always see me as just another interesting little conquest.

Tears stung her eyes with sudden, fierce pain. Don't cry! she told herself angrily. What's the matter with you? Can't you take it when a handsome, desirable, gorgeous, intelligent man like Jean-Luc Ferrat tries to seduce you every way he knows how? No, she thought, her mouth trembling. I *can't* take it. I'm too close to love. . .

Moving back from the wardrobe, she sank on to the bed. I'm almost in love, so nearly, so very nearly. . .how can I stop him taking my heart as well as my body? How can I stop him pursuing me?

What if there were another man involved with her? He would stop pursuing her then — wouldn't he? After all, there could have been. He had asked himself, were there any men in Paris who cared for her? The thought of any men in Paris caring for her was a joke, of course, as she well knew, because no man had ever visited her lonely flat in the Bois during those first two years, and when she'd moved in with Marie-Claire a few streets away the only men who came to visit were friends of Marie-Claire's, and no sexual threat whatsoever to Isabelle. After all, she was five years older than Marie-Claire. Their taste in men was different.

There was a knock at the door.

'Isabelle?' Jean-Luc knocked again, then came in, frowning when he saw her. 'You're not even dressed and it's seven-twenty!'

'I'm almost ready,' she said, staring at him, clutching the bath-towel protectively at her breasts. 'I was just trying to decide what to wear.'

He smiled and strode in, closing the door behind him. 'Let me choose!' He moved to her wardrobe.

'No!' Isabelle got to her feet, eyes filled with hot, angry determination. 'You've been dominating me for long enough, Jean-Luc, and I won't let you get away with it any more!'

He turned to look down at her, devastatingly handsome in a dark Armani suit, his jaw freshly shaven, the strong sensuality of his firm mouth making her pulses quiver.

'Have I been dominating you, Isabelle?' he said softly.

'Yes.'

'And I thought I was initiating you in the arts of the senses,' he murmured teasingly, his smile making her heart turn over with love.

'Whatever you were doing,' she said huskily, 'I want it to stop, and I've spent the afternoon thinking long and hard about it.'

'Well, don't just stand there, quivering; tell me what you've decided.'

'To find another man!' she said, lifting her bright head.

There was a brief, tense silence.

'What?' he said between his teeth.

'To find another man. I think that's my only option now, Jean-Luc, to make you see that I really do not want our relationship to contin——'

'You think I'd let you take another man?' he said roughly under his breath. 'After all the work I've done, you think I'd step back and watch him get everything I've begun to set free?' His hard hands took her shoulders. 'Think again, *chérie*! If I catch you anywhere near another man, I'll take you straight to bed, no mercy, no get-out clauses, and make damned sure I get what I've been working so hard for!'

Her mouth shook. 'But you can't do this, Jean-Luc! It isn't fair; I have a right to be free, and to choose another man—someone who might love me! You've made it clear enough that you don't, and never will, love me. So why shouldn't I look for someone else?'

'This is because of that conversation on the cliff, isn't it?' he bit out thickly, staring down at her.

'Isabelle — I didn't mean to hurt you when I said that about never loving you.'

Pride stung her. 'I wasn't hurt. I'm still not hurt!'

'I can see that you are.' His hands bit into her shoulders. 'Now, listen, *chérie*. We agreed I was going to rebuild your confidence —— '

'We didn't agree! You simply took the matter into your own hands!'

'And there it remains. I'm not going to allow you to take another man. There'll be trouble if you even attempt it. I've been patient with you so far, but if I see you trying to get someone else I'll get very angry indeed. Angrier than you can imagine.'

'You can't stop me, Jean-Luc. I shall start going out with Marie-Claire again, and keep away from you. Maybe then I'll meet a man who —— '

'No!'

'Yes, Jean-Luc, I want another man who —— '

'*No!*' he bit out hoarsely. 'My God, are you trying to drive me completely out of my mind? Don't you know that I'll go crazy if I see you with another man? How can you even consider —— ?'

'But how can I consider anything else!' she burst out in frustration. 'You're pushing me into an involvement that can only be described as dangerous! And how can you, Jean-Luc, when you know the only other man I've ever been involved with broke my heart?'

'Anthony didn't break your heart,' he bit out suddenly, breathing hard. 'He broke your confidence, your trust, your self-esteem — but not your heart, because you never gave it to him.'

She flinched, appalled by the truth of that and unable to admit it.

'You didn't love Anthony. Did you?'

'I did love him, I —— '

'No, you didn't! You were young and selfish. You had no idea whát love was and you married that boy because you liked the image he reflected of your own radiant glory.'

She flinched again, her voice shaking. 'No. . .! That's a wicked thing to say! You have no right to say such things!'

'You never loved him!' he bit out brutally.

'Oh, God. . .' She tried to get past him.

He pulled her back, hands hard, saying raggedly,, 'You stay where you are and listen to the truth, damn it!'

'No!' Her voice was hoarse with years of terrible guilt. 'I did love Anthony, I did; I was young but I ——'

'No!' He was breathing hard. 'You were incapable of true love. You never loved him and he knew it. That's precisely why he wanted to hurt you so much, and why he was eventually able to destroy you.'

Her mouth shook. Tears stung her eyes.

'It's true, isn't it?' he said ruthlessly. 'You married him on a fairy-tale that didn't exist, and your whole world collapsed when the fairy-tale was ripped back to reveal a real man who was a stranger to your selfish, spoiled, wilful little heart.'

With a hoarse sob, she buried her face in her hands, crying uncontrollably, devastated by the appalling truth in his words, a truth she had never admitted to anyone else. The guilt she had felt for three years came flooding out in unstoppable tears. She had never really loved Anthony at all. She had married him and made the last year of his life a year without real love. Oh, how could she live with the guilt of it, the terrible, terrible guilt?

'All right,' he said suddenly, gently, touching her

neck, the back of her hair, his voice deep and rough with emotion. 'Come here. . .'

Isabelle whispered thickly, 'Don't hold me. . . I'm so ashamed. . .'

'It's OK.' His arms went around her, stroking her hair. 'There's no reason to be ashamed. It wasn't your fault, Isabelle. You were very young, and your only experience of love was with your father, a man who loved and indulged you to the point of being besotted.' He laughed softly, kissing her tear-stained cheek. 'He has a lot to answer for! But *you* don't. It wasn't your fault Anthony got drunk that night. It wasn't your fault he crashed and killed himself. You feel guilty because you didn't love him and now he's dead. People always feel like that when somebody dies. And there's very little you can do except live with it.'

'But I should have loved him,' she whispered hoarsely, clinging to his broad shoulders. 'I should have loved him!'

'Well, you can love him now.' He drew back, eyeing her. 'Hmm? Plenty of forgiveness all round. Forgive him, forgive yourself — and then just smile and wave goodbye to Anthony.' He watched the tears flowing down her cheeks, then pulled her back into his power-ful arms. 'Shh! Don't cry. I knew it already. I just wanted to make sure it was said.'

'No man has ever loved me.' The words spilled out of her. 'No one ever will because ——'

'*Chérie*, you're talking nonsense now,' he said deeply, stroking her hair, holding her against his powerful chest. 'Is this the way you've been thinking in Paris for three years? That no one would ever love you because of what you'd done?'

'Yes. . .!' She nodded, crying harder. 'All the time, I thought it all the time, and I still think it, I ——'

'Ah, Isabelle!' He took her hands, and kissed her tears. 'You will find love, and sooner than you think. But you must be honest with the man who eventually gives you love in return for yours. A market-place, *chérie*. Remember?'

She stared at him, tearful and confused, trying to understand. A smile touched his hard mouth. 'And this is the last thorn I had to pull out of your heart. . .your angry little heart. Your feelings for Anthony were always complex. You tried to pretend they were simple. It is so dangerous to pretend — as you have found out.' He kissed her, again. 'Now you really must get dressed. We're going to be late, and this is Marie-Claire's evening. We can discuss this later tonight, when we get home.' He walked to the door, and threw her a lazy, seductive smile. 'We can discuss it in bed together. I'll look forward to it!'

Isabelle caught her breath as the door closed behind him.

Oh, my God, she thought in horror. He listened to all of that, watched me cry, hit me ruthlessly with terrible, unacceptable truths — and all to get me into bed with him? What am I going to do? she thought in terror. He's so dangerous he's almost inhuman.

CHAPTER SEVEN

THE white open-topped Rolls-Royce Corniche sped along the Avenue Princesse-Grace. It was sunset, the sky red-gold over Monte-Carlo, and the sea burnt like blue fire as the sun-bleached buildings on the left bathed in the warm orange glow. It was a wide open, cosmopolitan view made all the more exhilarating by the warm breeze flickering Isabelle's red-gold hair around her face like the fingers of freedom. But she was beginning to realise she had left it too late to build a fortress around her heart and prevent Jean-Luc Ferrat gaining entry. She could hardly believe that after a conversation so deep, so personal and so emotional he could start talking about sex again the minute it was over. Did he really feel so unaffected by what they'd discussed?

He was sitting in the back with her, devastatingly attractive in a black Armani suit, his jacket off, black waistcoat fitting tightly to his hard chest as his dark hair rippled around his strong face.

'By the way, I'd like you to meet me for lunch again tomorrow,' he said as they sped along towards the outer limits of Monte-Carlo. 'It's the Red Cross Ball tomorrow night. The most glittering event in the Monégasque calendar. I want to buy you a beautiful ballgown.'

'I already have a suitable evening dress to wear.' She shook her head, eyes resentful. 'And I don't want you to buy me any more presents.'

'Isabelle, don't spoil my surprises! I want to buy you

a dress, and I want to help you select it. It will be fun
for me. Come on — '

'No,' she said tightly, 'I'm not your mistress — I'm
your sister's friend and it would be most inappropriate
for you to buy me any more presents like that.'

'I could always bring pressure to bear,' he drawled,
his breath fanning her neck as he nibbled the sensitive
lobe of her ear.

'No! Look — I don't like the way you're always
talking about sex, thinking about it, putting it above
and before anything else — even deep emotional discussions, like the one we had just an hour or so ago!'

He studied her for a moment, then his long hand
touched her thigh. '*Chérie*. . . I know you've had a
strenuous emotional day. And I know that everything
we discussed today was very personal. But I want you
so much, I can barely stop myself from thinking about
making love to you. Don't hate me just because I
dwell on our moments of sensuality. They're so
intense. . .'

'They're too intense, and I want them to stop!' She
dashed his hand away, pain in her eyes. 'I stand by
what I said earlier tonight — I'm going to start looking
for a new man!'

His smile faded, mouth whitening as he studied her.
The warm breeze blew his black hair around his tanned
forehead. Rage glittered like black fire in his eyes.

'If I catch you anywhere near another man,' he said
thickly, 'I'll make you very sorry you ever tried to
double-cross me!'

'It's hardly double-crossing!'

'It is in my book! You know how I feel about you!'

'No. . .no, I don't!'

'I'm obsessed with you!' he said unsteadily, dark
colour invading his face.

Isabelle's heart skipped ragged beats. Hope flared in her, but the fear was so strong, the fear of being hurt, of being made to feel a fool, and the combination left her face white with taut, suppressed emotion.

'You must have known it from the beginning,' Jean-Luc said thickly. 'I can't keep away from you for five seconds. I've done all the running in this. My God, I've chased you — I sometimes think you enjoy telling me to go to hell, because you're curious to see if it sharpens my appetitie.'

'Your appetite for what?' she asked bitterly. 'Sex?'

His black lashes flickered on tough cheekbones. He studied her for a long moment, some indecipherable emotion blazing in his dark eyes. Then his mouth gave a hard, cynical twist. 'What else?'

She looked away. It hurt to look at him. All she could do was stare straight ahead at the gleaming lights of Monte-Carlo on the Avenue Princesse-Grace and watch them begin to blur. 'I thought for a minute you were going to tell me you had — deeper feelings that lust for me.'

He studied her white profile intently. 'But didn't we discuss that this afternoon? The market-place, remember, *chérie*? Love for love. No other deal is possible.' His strong hand touched her cheek. 'At least, not where I'm concerned.'

She flicked bitter green eyes at him. 'Love isn't a deal, Jean-Luc! You either love someone or you don't. There's no guarantee you'll get love in return just because you happen to feel it for someone!'

'Ah. . .' he said softly. 'Now we're getting somewhere.'

Isabelle stared at him in confusion, her lips parted. What on earth did he mean by that? She was just going to ask him when the Rolls slid up outside the Monte-Carlo Beach Hotel.

'We're here,' Jean-Luc said coolly. 'Don't forget this is Marie-Claire's evening. I've stolen you away from her. The least we can do is make sure she has a good time tonight. So don't let her see the extent of our own very personal conflict.'

Isabelle nodded, then stepped out and smoothed down the fitted red velvet of her dress, strapless and sexy against the blaze of her red-gold hair. Jean-Luc watched her with a cool smile, his eyes veiled.

'By the way,' he murmured, pulling her towards him and kissing her cheek, 'you look lovely.'

Her heart skipped with desire and pain as she returned his kiss, her eyes briefly closing, leaning against his powerful body, trying to come to terms with her own rocketing feelings of love towards him. A second later he had released her, and they walked into the Beach Hotel.

'Monsieur Ferrat!' The *maître d'* welcomed them effusively as they entered the glittering, open-air restaurant. 'Wonderful to see you again! Allow me to show you to your table. . .'

Jean-Luc strode coolly across the restaurant and women stared in admiration at his savagely handsome face, the masculine prowl of his arrogant walk; and Isabelle's veins ran with jealousy and pain because although she was with him he was not hers, and never would be. He belonged only to himself, this devastatingly attractive and intelligent man who was slowly but surely introducing her to the first real feelings of love she had ever had for a man.

'Jean-Luc!' Marie-Claire's eight friends all smiled and waved.

'*Ça va!*'

'Beep-beep, *c'est le weekend*!'

They sat at a large table by the illuminated pool. Fairy-lights were hung from tall palm trees. The whole ambience was hot, glamorous and very Monte-Carlo.

'Big brother! I thought you'd never get here!'

'Are we late?' Jean-Luc frowned, glancing at his watch.

'No, but I know what you and Isabelle are like! Always disappearing into rooms — laughing and kissing and talking together! *Vive l'amour*!'

Isabelle went scarlet, felt her eyes dart to Jean-Luc.

But Jean-Luc just drawled sardonically, 'Take no notice of my very indiscreet sister, who will get her ears soundly boxed as soon as we are home! Sit down, *chérie*. . .let me introduce you to this noisy bunch.' He held a chair out for her, and took the seat beside her, one powerful arm flung out along the back of her chair to signify his male territorial possession of her while his long legs were crossed towards her body.

'Speak to us in American, Isabelle!' a beautiful Monégasque girl called Fabienne said. 'Just like in the movies!'

'Well, I really don't know what to say, y'all!' she said in her Louisiana voice.

They all roared with laughter.

'*Mon Dieu*!' Marie-Claire's boyfriend, Olivier, smacked his forehead. 'Scarlett O'Hara! Say — *demain est un autre jour*!'

'Tomorrow is another day!' she said thickly, looking at Jean-Luc through her golden lashes and seeing the smile on his tough mouth as they both exchanged private memories of that conversation this afternoon.

The waiter appeared. 'Are you ready to order?'

They all rapidly studied their menus. Isabelle chose

pasta *aux fruits de mer*. Jean-Luc ordered his usual
plain fare — *filet de boeuf* cooked *à point*.

'*Et cinq bouteilles de Châteauneuf-du-Pape*,' he
drawled as the order ended, and studied the young
men and women around the table. 'You're not all
driving, I take it?'

They all laughed and pointed at two young men,
who grimaced. 'We lost the toss of a ten-franc piece!'

'Five bottles, then.'

Everyone cheered. 'Good old Jean-Luc!'

'Make the most of it,' he drawled, brows arching.
'It'll be a long time before I take you lot out to dinner
again.'

They all booed.

He laughed and shook his head. 'The company you
keep, Marie-Claire!'

Isabelle listened to the good-natured repartee and
felt so hurt, so terribly shut out, because she knew
suddenly that these people would know him all their
lives, whereas she would know him only until he had
seduced her, and then she would never be at his table
again.

Their meal arrived.

'So what do you think of Monaco, Isabelle?'
Fabienne asked her.

She looked up, trying to sound cheerful, and said, 'I
fell in love with it at first sight.'

Jean-Luc pushed his plate away, barely touched,
and flicked a dark look at Isabelle from below those
hooded lids.

'We arrived in big brother's helicopter!' Marie-
Claire said. 'The best view, of course.'

'Ah, yes!' Everyone around the table nodded. 'You
can see everything from the air. It isn't split in two as
much as it is when you're living here.'

'Yes,' Isabelle said slowly, 'the old and the new. It is quite split, isn't it? The ancient medieval streets, the Prince's Palace, the struggle for conquest on the rock. . .'

'While Monte-Carlo,' said Jean-Luc softly, 'glitters down here in all its modern, hedonistic glory!'

'That's right!' She studied him. 'I love both sides, though. I think they're equally attractive.'

'*C'est l'amour*,' Jean-Luc said thickly. 'One cannot love just a piece here or a piece there. One either loves the whole sum of the parts, for good or bad, or one does not truly love.'

Isabelle studied his handsome face, her eyes startled, thinking of him tearing her mask off, picking her heart to pieces and pointing to each one. Seductress. Flirt. Selfish little heartbreaker. Frightened, hurt little girl. And damaged, broken woman in desperate need of help that only he could give.

He's got to love me, she thought in panic. No one else ever will, no one else ever could. Please love me, please. . .

'So. . .' he said under his breath, arching dark brows. 'You fell in love with Monaco at first sight?'

'Yes. . .' She couldn't look away, her heart beating with sudden wild hope. 'Although I didn't realise it at the time.'

His dark eyes were riveted to her face. The others seemed to fade away from them, leaving them locked into that dark, private world they shared. Then he looked coolly away, and the moment was shattered, no longer an exchange of personal emotion, but just another twist in the devastatingly skilful Jean-Luc seduction technique.

Fabienne said, 'But tomorrow is the big night! The

highlight of the season! The Monaco Red Cross Ball, and everyone will be there!'

'But the crucial question,' Marie-Claire laughed, 'is what is every woman going to *wear*!'

Everyone laughed uproariously.

'I'm taking Isabelle out tomorrow,' Jean-Luc drawled coolly, 'to buy her the most beautiful ballgown in town.'

'Unfair!' Fabienne cried. 'Oh, you lucky girl!'

'I wonder,' Marie-Claire said suddenly, 'who Michel Balanchine will be taking to the ball tomorrow?'

Jean-Luc tensed, and flicked his cool dark eyes across the restaurant at a man who was just arriving, attracting attention with his cool, arrogant walk and his impressive height, strikingly handsome in a smart black evening suit.

'He's coming this way!' Fabienne murmured, looking quickly at Jean-Luc. 'I bet he stops at the table, just to annoy you.'

'I bet he does!' drawled Jean-Luc. 'I sometimes wonder just how desperate he is to get the better of me.'

'Desperate,' Marie-Claire said with a bite.

Jean-Luc's jet-black eyes narrowed and he started tapping his foot.

Isabelle was just wondering what the hell was going on when she felt a hand slide strokingly over her red-gold hair, one long finger touching her bare neck.

Gasping, she turned around to see Michel Balanchine murmuring, 'Jean-Luc! Introduce me to this astonishingly beautiful stranger!'

'I might consider it if you take your hand off her neck!' Jean-Luc drawled in a voice like a razor.

Tension prickled over the table.

Balanchine smiled and removed his hand. 'Forgive

me. Such lovely hair! And such an unusual colour for *une Monégasque*. Are you, in fact, *une éstrangère, mademoiselle?*'

Isabelle's lashes flickered. '*Oui, je suis américaine.*'

His smile widened. '*Américaine*? From which state?'

'Louisiana,' drawled Jean-Luc beside her. 'Her name is Isabelle Montranix, and she is staying at my apartment.'

Isabelle tensed angrily, her face flaming. He had practically told the man that she was his mistress! Did he have no regard for her self-respect? Turning to Michel Balanchine, she said tightly, 'As a matter of fact, I'm Marie-Claire's friend. We met in Paris.'

Jean-Luc's hand bit into her shoulder and the people at the table exchanged tense glances while Marie-Claire went very pale.

'*Vraiment. . .?*' Michel Balanchine flicked amused blue eyes to Jean-Luc's hard face, and gave a slow, cynical smile. 'Marie-Claire's friend from Paris? How is Paris? My favourite city. May I join you?'

Jean-Luc said coolly, 'Surely you are dining with someone tonight, Balanchine? We wouldn't want to deprive your guest of the pleasure——'

'I'm dining with a business colleague.' Balanchine smiled smoothly. 'He's not here yet. You wouldn't want me to sit alone when I could join your table and speak to such a beautiful lady, would you?'

'Of course not,' Jean-Luc said in a cool, menacing voice, then beckoned to a waiter, saying curtly, 'Bring a chair for Balanchine and serve the coffee. We'll be leaving shortly.'

Michel Balanchine sank down, smiling at Isabelle. 'What were you doing in Paris, *mademoiselle*?'

'Working and living,' she said politely. 'I left

Louisiana three years ago. I'm half French, you understand. I was drawn to France.'

He smiled and sighed. 'I've always wanted to visit Louisiana! New Orleans fascinates me. Is that where you lived? Oh, tell me about it!'

She told him about her parents' big old Georgian-style manor just outside New Orleans, about the long, hot days and how she missed the sound of crickets and cicadas, the moths as big as hummingbirds, and the taste of her mama's home-made lemonade on a swelteringly humid day.

'I sometimes miss it,' she concluded, 'but I feel so at home——'

'*Chérie*,' Jean-Luc interrupted coolly, his voice deliberately intimate, 'would you like a liqueur? Cointreau? Grand Marnier?'

She shook her red-gold head, murmuring, 'No, thank you. Michel, would you like something?'

Jean-Luc's fingers bit into her arm. 'Just the bill, then!' he said tightly to the waiter.

'You are leaving so soon?' Balanchine protested.

'Yes, we're all going to the casino to——'

'Isabelle,' Jean-Luc said tightly, 'finish your coffee!'

The bill arrived in a flash and Jean-Luc signed the Am-Ex chit, getting to his feet, his hand taking Isabelle by the wrist and lifting her to her feet beside him.

'Goodbye, Balanchine!' he drawled as he strode past the man. 'No doubt we'll see you at the Red Cross Ball tomorrow night!'

Goodbyes were called as their party walked back across the sun-bleached terrace, lit by floodlights and fairy-lights, the sky completely dark now and filled with a thousand stars.

Outside, Marie-Claire and her friends climbed into two cars. 'See you at the casino, Jean-Luc?'

'No,' he said coolly, bending his head to the window. 'We'll head for home now. But you have a good time. See you in the morning.'

He stood a few feet from the Rolls, waving a cool hand in greeting as the other two cars sped off, going beep-beep and blaring out loud pop music.

Then he turned to Isabelle, his eyes blazing, and bit out thickly, 'You little bitch! How dare you sit and flirt with that bastard all night? How dare you do that to me in front of —— ?'

'I didn't flirt with him!' she said in angry amazement. 'What do you mean — flirt with him? I just talked to the man, that's all!'

'You heard what we said when he first appeared.' His mouth shook. 'You knew he was my enemy! Yet you deliberately flirted with him, encouraged him to sit at the table, talked to him about New Orleans when he wasn't remotely interested!' He stared down at her, his face furious. 'My God, if I didn't want you so much, I'd throw you into his arms and say good riddance to you!'

Pain struck her so deeply she went white, saying hoarsely, 'Yes, that's about what I'd expect from you! Passing me around like a — what was it, Jean-Luc? A Christmas present?' Her mouth shook. 'I hate your guts! I wish I'd never laid eyes on you! I wish I'd —— '

'The feeling was very mutual ten minutes ago!' he bit out. 'You really know how to stick the knife in, don't you? What was it, Isabelle? Revenge for our little conversation on the cliff?'

'Don't try to pretend you don't know why I talked to him! You practically told the man I was your lover! You did it deliberately! You wanted him to think I was staying at your apartment — as your mistress!'

His face ran with angry colour. 'I said that because I

wanted to make sure he didn't try to touch you! It never occurred to me that you might be the one to encourage him!'

'That's because you didn't think about me or my feelings.' Her voice shook. 'You just said it, in front of all those people, and made me feel like a whore!'

'I wasn't thinking clearly,' he said hoarsely, raking a hand through his dark hair. 'I'm not perfect, I can't get it right all the time. Why didn't you just wait and speak to me about it privately instead of flirting with him? Did it have to be so public? Did you have to pick him? And all that on top of what you said earlier, about finding another man! That's why you did it, isn't it? You saw the hostility between me and Balanchine, so you decided to pick him to be your lover, not me!' His eyes were murderously black. 'My God, I'll kill you if you try to replace me with him!'

She stared, suddenly shocked by the violence of his rage; the fury he was showing went beyond anything she had ever seen in him, and suddenly she thought, Why is he angry just because I talked to that man?

'Why are you so angry?' she asked in a slow voice of dawning awareness. 'What has that man done to you in the past?'

His eyes grew savage. A muscle jerked in his cheek. In a slurred voice he bit out, 'Mind your own business!'

She caught her breath as though he'd slapped her. 'You can say that to me?' she demanded hoarsely. 'After everything I've told you? Every personal detail, every question about my past answered? And when I ask you one personal question you tell me to mind my own business?'

'That's right!' he said under his breath. 'Mind your own business!'

Her mouth shook. What he was really saying was,

You mean aboslutely nothing to me, Isabelle. Absolutely nothing. It hurt so much to hear it that she was incapable of speech for a few painful seconds.

Jean-Luc watched her with intense eyes. 'I never want to catch you talking to Balanchine again. And I want your word on that, Isabelle. Or the reprisals will be more unpleasant than you could ever dream.'

'But you won't tell me why. You make a scene like this, says hurtful things to me, and then demand that I never speak to a perfect stranger again — but you won't tell me why.'

'Yes, those are the facts, Isabelle! Now give me your word or I'll take you straight home to bed and give you what you apparently intend my biggest enemy to get instead of me!'

'All right!' she said hoarsely, her mouth shaking with emotion. 'I promise never to speak to him again! There! Are you satisfied? Will you stop hurling insults and vile threats at me now?'

He stood there, breathing hard, and the lights of the Monte-Carlo Beach Hotel illuminated the hard plains of his passionate face. 'You'd better keep to that promise, Isabelle.'

Her eyes burned with bitter tears. 'Of course I'll keep to it! What choice do I have? If I don't you'll only carry out your disgusting threat! But why should I even be surprised you had the gall to make it? Your only interest in me has always been sex, and now you're making it brutally clear that all our personal discussions have been nothing but a way to get me into bed. I began to think you might really be interested in what had happened to me. I began to think you might actually care that I'd been so badly hurt. But I was a fool even to consider that. Your intention all along has been to dress me up like a whore, seduce me, and then throw me out of the principality once you've sated your lust!'

'I didn't say that, I never said that; don't twist my words, Isabelle, don't ——' he shouted hoarsely, and suddenly his hand shot back from her wrist to take her by the shoulders and shake her, but Isabelle thought he was going to hit her and she flinched in unconscious anticipation of a blow. 'Don't twist my words. . .' his dark voice whispered as he watched her flinch away from him, her hands over her head.

Silence. Nothing but the sounds of the crickets in the hot night and the sea lapping gently at the dark beach.

'Why did you do that?' he demanded in a shaking voice, staring, black emotion in his eyes. 'Why did you flinch like a frightened child?'

'I didn't!' Her face was averted, her voice low.

'You thought I was going to hit you. . .' He stared with horror. 'Did he do that? Did that man you married hit you?'

'I don't want to talk about it, and I wouldn't tell you anyway—not after what you just said to me!'

'Did he hit you?' Jean-Luc demanded hoarsely. 'Tell me, Isabelle! I insist that you ——'

'Mind your own business!' she flung through her teeth, eyes stinging with bitter tears.

He went white. Isabelle looked away again, biting her lip, struggling not to cry.

Jean-Luc ran a hand through his dark hair, his fingers tight on her wrist. Then he said thickly, 'All right! I've got the promise I wanted from you. Just make sure you stick to it, and never speak to that little creep Balanchine again.' He turned to walk back to the car. 'Now, let's go home.'

'So you can take me to bed?' Her voice trembled as

she dug her high heels in and refused to move though he pulled at her wrist. 'No! I won't go! Take me to a hotel! I can't stand this any more! I want to leave Monaco, leave the apartment, leave ——'

'You will not leave!' he said under his breath. 'I've told you before — if you try to get away from me, I'll follow and bring you back.'

'I won't stay here!'

'You want a long tug of war — is that it?' His voice shook. 'If that's what you want, you'll get it! I've put too much time and effort into you to stop now, so don't try to fight me, Isabelle, because I *will* have you, and on my terms!' His hand tightened on her wrist. 'Now get in the car! You're coming home with me!'

Isabelle looked at him, her eyes blurring with tears. What choice did she have? She couldn't run from him like this, with no money, no passport, no cheque-book or credit card. They were all in the apartment, with the rest of her things.

'Are you going to try and take me tonight?' she asked thickly, lifting her bright head. 'If you do, Jean-Luc, I'll fight you till ——'

'No,' he said thickly. 'I don't want you tonight. Not after the way you just behaved with Balanchine. Now, just get in the car. It's been a long day and tomorrow will be even longer.'

He strode to the car and she went with him, her face bleached white as she got in beside him and the car pulled away.

Monte-Carlo's fabulous night-time glamour shone across the horizon, the buildings lit up like a cosmopolitan city while the black mounts of Mont Agel and Tête de Chien rose behind it like dark protectors.

They drove in tense, bitter silence. Isabelle couldn't look at him; it hurt too much to remember how he had spoken to her just now, and the hot breeze flickered her red-gold hair around her hurt, white face.

When they got back to the apartment, she rode up in the lift with him, feeling so insignificant that she didn't even consider asking him again why Balanchine obviously triggered such a violent response, although she wanted badly to know; but how could she ask again, when he had already told her so cuttingly to mind her own business? Her own business. . . God, how could he say that? After everything she'd told him. Revealing layer after layer of her private despair — and all Jean-Luc revealed to her was his charm and seduction techniques, two facets of his character that were so impersonal as to be an insult.

'I'm going to bed,' he said icily when they walked into the silent apartment. 'I suggest you do the same. And don't think about leaving in the middle of the night, *chérie* — ' he said the word '*chérie*' with biting contempt ' — or you'll feel the full weight of my anger when I am forced to bring you back and teach you who is master in this relationship.'

He didn't even say goodnight, just walked into his bedroom and slammed the door.

Isabelle stood there in silence as though nailed to the floor, and felt her heart crack. . .

CHAPTER EIGHT

I'M IN love with him. . . .

Isabelle's eyes closed on a wave of overwhelming pain and she groped blindly for her bedroom door, going in, shutting it behind her and leaning on it, drawing in her breath as the room swam in and out, in and out. . . .

'Oh, my God. . .!' Her hands went to her face, covering it shakingly, and she wanted to sink on to the floor, crying, because it was too late now, she had lost the fight; she was in love with him, so deeply in love that she could no longer think properly; but she had to think, she had to try to salvage what was left of her heart before he did exactly what he'd said he would do: break it into tiny pieces and scatter it to the Mistral. Love, admiration, respect, hatred and sexual desire. . .so closely intermingled. . .roaring up at her like fire, flooding her veins and telling her this was the one she had waited for, the only man she could ever love, the only man she probably would ever love.

She felt such a fool. How could she have reached this point when she had fought so hard. . .? No wonder I hated him on sight, she thought with a hoarse laugh. I knew, from the very minute I saw him, that I'd fall in love with him unless I fought for my life against him.

Suddenly, everything made sense, everything, every incident, every reaction, every second of her life since she had seen him drive up at Nice airport and get out of the car, sliding his dark glasses off to stare at her in

the sunlight. . .the way she'd prickled from head to
foot, snapped at him, hated him like poison and gone
out of her way to avoid him, even when he forced her
to recognise the extent and very dangerous nature of
her desire for him.

That desire had been the tip of the iceberg, and
underneath she now felt the whole vast dark mass
dredge up from her heart and mind to show her love.
She felt capsized in her little boat before it.

Isabelle stumbled out of her clothes with a sudden
need to be busy, to move about, not to think, as
though somehow her love would go away if she did
that, somehow the pain would stop seeping across her
heart, saturating it in the agony of unrequited love. . .

Suddenly she had to sit down, legs shaking, naked,
her nightdress in her hands and her heart banging with
horror. What am I going to do? She stared at her
nightdress fixedly as though it could tell her the
answer. I recovered from Anthony, just, only just —
but I'll never recover from Jean-Luc Ferrat. How can
I? The reason I was able to recover from Anthony in
the end was because I was never truly in love with
him. But I am in love with Jean-Luc. Look at
me. . .shaking from head to foot, in love for the first
time and helpless to do anything about it, even though
I know I'll get nothing from him, nothing, just a few
nights of love if I'm lucky.

It was quite some time before she realised she was
still clutching her nightdress in her hands, staring
unseeingly at it. Then she slowly pulled it on and got
into bed. She put the light out, but it was a long time
before she went to sleep.

Sunlight streamed through her balcony doors, and
she felt a dark presence in the room as she sleepily

turned over, her eyes flickering open to look vaguely upwards.

Her heart stopped beating and felt as though it bled.

Jean-Luc was here, watching her, his face hard as he sat on the bed, impeccably dressed in another of his business suits, formal, formidable, tight waistcoat, crisp white cuffs, gold cufflinks and rich silk tie.

'Good morning,' he said flatly.

There was a tense pause.

'Good morning.' She answered, her face taut with pain and pride. Her hands clutched the duvet. She couldn't think of anything else to say.

'I came to remind you that we have a lunch date.' He was expressionless. 'I'm buying you a ballgown — remember?'

'I don't want a ballgown, thank you,' she said with sudden shaking anger, then looked sharply away, her mouth trembling as tears stung.

Jean-Luc's hand caught her chin, forced her to look at him. The dark eyes inspected her. They lingered on the dark circles beneath her eyes, and slowly softened. 'You're hurt,' he said unsteadily. 'Was I very cruel to you?'

'I don't want to discuss it!' She pushed his hand away.

'I didn't bother to explain last night,' he said thickly, still watching her. 'I was too angry with you. But if you still want an explanation, I'll give you one. So here's your chance. Ask for it.'

'No!' she said thickly, blinking her tears back.

'You're being childish.'

'I can be childish if I want to!' she flung.

Jean-Luc laughed softly, and the charm in his face made her heart spin dizzily over and over and over into his pocket.

Breathless, she just stared at him. The laughter died, emotion flaring violently between them, and as his smile faded he lowered his gaze from hers.

'*Chérie*,' he said huskily, touching her red-gold hair with long fingers, 'I can see I made you cry yourself to sleep.'

'No, you didn't!' she denied in angry confusion.

He flicked his gaze up. 'Your eyes are swollen and bruised.'

'No, they're not.'

'Hmm.' A hard smile touched his mouth, his dark eyes watching hers. 'Well, we will go ahead with the day as planned. I want you to meet me at my hotel at midday. I'll telephone the boutique when I get to work and arrange an appointment for us, so be punctual, please.'

'I don't want a ballgown, Jean-Luc,' she said angrily, 'and I won't accept one from you!'

'Don't argue with me, *chérie*! I'm late as it is, and I detest being undisciplined where my work is concerned.' He bent his dark head and kissed her mouth briefly, a blaze of emotion in his kiss that made her heart somersault and her hands flutter up to his strong neck, love in her smothered gasp of pleasure.

He lifted his mouth from hers, and his face was flushed as he said thickly, 'Now accept that I'm not going to change my mind, and arrive at my hotel at midday.' He got to his feet. 'Remember to wear something you can easily slip in and out of. You might have to try a lot of dresses before we find the right one.'

She just glared at him in bitter silence.

'And don't bring that mutinous little face with you,' he murmured. 'I want to see you looking beautiful, not glaring at me like a red-haired witch! Also remember——' he raised one long hand '—we will be in public. I don't want the sales ladies of the boutique gossiping about the hostility between Jean-Luc Ferrat and his lovely Américaine.'

'I'll do my best!' she said tightly.

'I hope you will, *chérie*, because I detest my personal life being placed in the public spotlight.'

'Then why have you lived as you have?.'

'There's a difference between my public persona and my personal life.'

'Not from what I've experienced so far!' she said tautly. 'If anything, you're more dangerous to women than the Press say you are!'

He laughed under his breath, dark eyes glittering. 'Am I, *chérie*? How flattering to hear you say it.'

She coloured angrily and looked away, changing the subject. 'But I feel the same as you when it comes to bad behaviour in public. So, regardless of how much I hate you and would dearly like to tear this ballgown up and fling it in your face——' her voice shook as she finished tightly '—I will behave as you ask, and not let the sales ladies see my feelings.'

A hard smile touched his cynical mouth. 'Good.'

'But it doesn't mean I don't feel them.' Her eyes hated him.

'Quite, *chérie*,' he murmured sardonically. 'But you hardly need explain the finer points of public image to me. It is a system I have learned to live with on an international level, as you will find out tonight when we arrive at the Ball.' He glanced at the Rolex on his dark-haired wrist. 'And now I really must go to work. Midday, remember. And don't be late.' He strode to the door and went out, closing it coolly behind him.

Isabelle lay there for a long moment, thinking. . .brief snatches of conversation flashing through her mind.

'I will behave as you ask and not let the sales ladies see my feelings. But it doesn't mean I don't feel them.'

'Quite, *chérie*. But you hardly need explain. . . It is a system I have learned to lived with. . .'

Frowning, she knew there was something in there that she badly needed to hear. Was he saying that he had become an expert at disguising his true feelings? Of course he was! What else could he be saying? But that was only in public — surely? He couldn't possibly be expert at hiding his feelings in private, too. . .could he?

Typical woman-in-love thoughts, she chided herself angrily. How one lies to oneself when Cupid's arrow pierces the heart. Maybe the arrows were all dipped in blindness-potion, making the victims of love self-deceiving fools.

Pushing back the duvet, she looked at the clock and sighed, shaking her head. It was only ten to eight! She'd probably only got four or five hours' sleep, yet she felt wide awake, buzzing with adrenalin, living on love, unable to stop the drug flooding her bloodstream. She went out into the corridor, heading for the kitchen to see if Madame Dusort was up with a pot of fresh coffee made for Jean-Luc before he left for work.

'Morning!' Marie-Claire came padding sleepily out of her bedroom. 'I lost my watch last night. What time is it?'

'A few minutes before eight,' Isabelle told her.

'Ugh!' Marie-Claire wrinkled her nose. 'What on earth are you doing up at this ungodly hour? Oh. . .' Her lashes flickered then she smiled and said lightly, 'Has Jean-Luc just left for work?'

Isabelle felt her face flame. 'Well. . .yes.'

'Mmm.' Marie-Claire nodded, then said softly, 'Well, I went to the casino, then danced the night away. So I'm not getting up much before the crack of lunch.' She yawned sleepily. 'Night-night! Have a nice time buying your ballgown with big brother. . .'

The door closed and Isabelle was left feeling very odd indeed. Why was Marie-Claire so in favour of the relationship? Surely she should be angry with her brother? She must know Jean-Luc was only playing with her, and even though she couldn't possibly have interfered with his game she should surely show at least a little disapproval instead of such pleasure?

Isabelle was left to her own devices all morning. She took her coffee on the salon balcony, watching Monte-Carlo come alive as the warm white morning sun gradually turned to burning yellow and began to scorch the whole dazzling principality.

At a quarter to midday, she walked down to the Hotel Ferrat. Jean-Luc strode into the marble reception hall at the same moment as she walked through the swing glass doors.

'Very prompt!' he drawled with a careless smile, and bent to kiss her cheek briefly, then straightened. 'I see you left your mutiny at home. . .?

'No, I brought it with me,' she said under her breath with a dazzling smile, her eyes hating him. 'I'm just hiding it so I can throw it at you when nobody's looking!'

He laughed and kissed her again, then drawled. 'Let's go!'

He guided her out on to the hot white steps, the sea bright blue opposite, a windsurfer and a white yacht gliding by in the distance while the red and white flag of Monaco fluttered gaily in the hot breeze outside the Hotel Ferrat.

The boutique was on the Boulevard des Moulins, and as they walked through the vast smoked-glass doors into an air-conditioned luxury foyer Jean-Luc was greeted with the usual respect and admiration he commanded everywhere in Monaco and Europe.

They were shown to an upstairs room, where a vast stretch of white carpeted floor held two luxurious white sofas and a long row of pretty mirrors along the other side of the wall where the dressing-rooms were.

Models paraded slowly before them, while she sat tensely with Jean-Luc on a sofa, his strong arm flung out behind her head, his long legs crossed towards her, one foot tapping to an imaginary beat.

'That one,' he said softly, suddenly, pointing.

Isabelle's heart leapt with delight at the ravishing cream ballgown shimmering with gold threads, tight-waisted, with a low décolletage, and off-the-shoulder delicate miniature sleeves.

'Go and try it on,' he drawled coolly.

Isabelle got to her feet, heart thudding with rage as she walked coolly to the changing-rooms, aware that the sales ladies assumed she was his mistress and that this was a rich man's gift to his expensive whore. God, she hated him for doing this to her. She would have liked to tear the ballgown up and throw it in his face in front of these women. But of course she didn't. She simply put it on, let the women zip her up and fuss over her, then walked out in a rustle of silk taffeta to parade before him with a smile of pure hatred.

He caught his breath as she walked out.

There was a silence as his dark eyes raced over her, his hard mouth parted, staring as the light caught the gold threads and shimmered them all over her like a fairy-tale princess, her tiny waist emphasised by the tight bodice and full skirts below, her creamy breasts pushed up in sensual invitation, her shoulders bare, her slim arms made even more delicate by the tiny scraps of taffeta pretending to be sleeves; and the blaze of her long red-gold hair against the dress was simply stunning.

'*Chérie*,' Jean-Luc said thickly, 'you take my breath away.' He turned to the sales ladies and drawled coolly, 'We'll take the dress. Wrap it immediately. Isabelle, get changed. I have another appointment in ten minutes.'

Isabelle turned and went back to the changing-room, white with rage at his curt dismissal. She was surprised the sales ladies treated her with such respect. God only knew what they were thinking.

They left the boutique, went out on to the busy, crowded, traffic-packed street. The open-topped Rolls waited for them, the chauffeur reading *Nice-Matin*. He flicked it shut and started the car as Jean-Luc helped Isabelle into the back with her vast, expensive dress-box.

'It's exactly what I imagined you in,' Jean-Luc drawled as they pulled away into the slow-crawling traffic. 'We were lucky to find it.'

She looked at him with rage burning in her eyes., 'I'd like to cut it into tiny shreds with a pair of scissors and stuff it down your selfish throat!'

His lashes flickered briefly as he stared.

'Do you have any idea how those women looked at me?' Her voice shook. 'Well, do you?'

'Isabelle ——'

'Taking me in there, buying me this dress, choosing it yourself, ordering me around as though I were a professional whore!'

'Be quiet!' he said through his teeth, eyes black with

anger. 'I did not treat you that way! I simply bought a dress for you to wear to the ball tonight.'

'Well, I'm not going to the ball!'

'Yes, you are!' he bit out, hand closing over her wrist with biting fingers. 'And what's more you will wear that dress, smile at the paparazzi and be polite to me for the duration of the evening!'

'I refuse, Jean-Luc, to allow you to continue dragging me into this involvement!' she said in hoarse fury.

'Fine!' he said thickly. 'I'll take the afternoon off, take you to bed and give you the biggest present of all!'

Her face ran red and she looked away, her mouth bitter. What could she say in response to that? That she would refuse to make love with him? They both knew perfectly well that she'd never be able to refuse if he really decided to let her have it, full blast, every last sexual weapon trained on her mercilessly.

'That's better,' he said under his breath, watching her. 'Now stop fighting me, Isabelle. Remember the ill-treated racehorse facing that last hurdle, hmm?' One long hand touched her thigh. 'We're so close, *chérie*, that's why you're rearing up and trying to bolt. But don't let your fear get the better of you. Everything will be so clear tonight. Just trust me to guide you——'

'With your experienced hands!' she said bitterly, eyes blazing. 'Oh, yes, how could I forget those experienced hands?'

The car pulled up suddenly, outside the apartment.

'I'll be home at seven,' Jean-Luc murmured, leaning close to kiss her white cheek. 'Be ready to leave for the ball at a quarter to eight. And Isabelle. . .' She looked up, her eyes meeting his. 'Wear the cream lingerie underneath the gown.' His mouth brushed burningly over hers. 'The stockings will go well with it. So will the scent of Chanel No.5.'

She got out of the car and slammed the door, walking furiously to the apartment foyer, her heart twisting in agony. Leaning against the lift-wall as it rode up, she thought. He's going to try and make love to me tonight, after the ball. Oh, God. . .he doesn't care about me, not at all, not one little bit. This is what it's been about all along — just lust. She felt tears shimmering in her eyes, tried to blink them back, her mouth shaking, totally lost in her own overwhelming emotions for Jean-Luc.

Reaching the top floor, she went to the apartment, using the key Marie-Claire had given her, and went in.

'Is that you, Isabelle?' Marie-Claire called from the salon.

'Yes.' She went in and dropped her keys and the box on a creamy couch, avoiding her eyes, hiding her unshed tears. 'Did you have a good sleep?'

'Wonderful.' Marie-Claire looked at the box. 'What did my indulgent brother buy you? A ballgown? I must see. . .'

Isabelle handed her the box, her face averted, filled with pain.

'Oh, my God!' Marie-Claire's voice whispered as she pulled the ballgown from the box, standing up with it in her hands, full-length, staring at it.

Isabelle tried to smile. 'It — it was kind of him to buy it.'

'But it's so romantic!' Marie-Claire stared. 'I haven't known him do anything romantic for years!'

She turned, staring, her lips parted as she stared at the dress then at her friend and heard her raw voice ask, 'Really. . .?'

'Yes, really, Isabelle!' She stared at the dress. 'I

expected him to buy you something slinky. A sexy red tight-fitting gown, or something with black sequins. But this. . .oh, Isabelle, this is unprecedented.'

Isabelle looked back at the dress, her heart leaping with sudden wild hope. 'Really? I—I mean—really, Marie-Claire?'

Marie-Claire studied her for a second, then said, '*Chérie*, don't tell Jean-Luc I said any of that. He'll be furious.'

Isabelle was silent, eyes intense.

'But really—it's true.' Marie-Claire slowly handed her the dress back, a smile lighting her eyes. 'And you'll be the belle of the ball tonight on my handsome brother's arm.'

Isabelle went into her bedroom later, sitting on the bed, staring at the dress, and thinking, What she said can't be true. Yet it *is* a romantic dress. And if he feels romantic for the first time in years, then. . .oh, she didn't dare hope, didn't dare believe it, terrified to in case she was wrong, because the hurt would be devastating if she believed he felt romantic about her, only to find out it was a terrible, wicked lie and that he felt nothing but lust.

Isabelle got ready for the ball at six o'clock, and was drawn into the sensual world Jean-Luc had introduced her to, spending half an hour in a Chanel-scented bath, emerging with skin like satin to blow-dry her hair, walking nude around the bedroom, the fan whirring softly overhead as she scented her skin again with fine white dusting powder, enjoying the sensuality of the fluffy pom-pom, aware that her body was excited, her nipples erect as she dusted herself slowly, thinking of Jean-Luc suddenly, feeling his presence in the bedroom, as though he were lying on the bed watching her. She shivered with arousal, then found herself at the lingerie box, almost blindly sliding the cream silk lace briefs on, the long creamy stockings with lace tops that caressed her scented thighs. Lying to herself, telling herself she had not put them on so that Jean-Luc could enjoy her body in them, she went to the dressing-table, her heart thudding as she put on her make-up, her jewellery, and brushed her long red-gold hair.

Finally, she slid into the magnificent ballgown, zipping it up and staring at herself in the mirror with a leap of shock.

I look beautiful, she thought, reaching out a hand to the glass.

'Isabelle!' Jean-Luc knocked at the door sharply. 'We're going to be late, *chérie*! How soon can you be ready?'

Pulses leaping, she walked to the door and opened it.

He drew in his breath sharply, his dark eyes racing over her long red-gold hair, the coral-painted lips, the pearls at her ears and throat, the creamy swell of her breasts and silky, scented bare shoulders, and the fabulous, glittering, fairy-tale dress.

'*Chérie*.' His voice held a hoarse note as he slid his hands on to her waist and drew her against his hard body. 'You're so beautiful, so unbelievably beautiful!'

Her eyes stared drowningly into his because for the first time she believed that she was.

'I want to kiss you thoroughly, but I mustn't spoil your beautiful make-up. The scent of your skin is making me dizzy. . .are you wearing anything special under that gown?' He gave an unsteady laugh. 'Tell me you are. . .!'

She had to drag herself out of her sensual reverie. 'Jean-Luc, I'm only wearing this gown because you inisted! We both know that I don't want this relationship to continue.'

'I keep telling you it's too late,' he said thickly, 'and when we get back from the ball I'll show you exactly what I mean.'

Her heart leapt angrily. 'No! I won't let you take me! Not tonight, not ever!'

'Isabelle, if you don't want me to touch your skin, why have you scented it especially for me? Don't blush and look so angry! I want to make love to you, to give you pleasure, so much pleasure that you lose all reason, as you will tonight ——' his eyes darkened ' — when we make love after the ball.'

'No!' She tried to pull away from him. 'No, I won't let you do it! I won't let you take my self-respect and dignity by treating me like a —— '

'Ssh!' He was frowning, stroking her hair. 'Don't say it, *chérie*. A whore is the very last thing I will ever treat you as.'

'That's not true!'

'Don't you know it even yet?' he asked thickly, that darkness in his eyes making her heart turn over with love. 'How have I treated you? Think back. As a princess, a seductress, a lover, a woman and a friend.'

Uncertainty and fear flashed in her heart as she said huskily, 'You only want sex from me. Admit it. Stop trying to wrap it up in charm and flattery.'

'That's how you see it now,' he murmured with a hard smile, 'but after the ball everything will seem very different. Just you wait and see.' He smiled and kissed her, then drawled, 'Come on. We mustn't be late. Our royal family will be there, and we must not appear discourteous.'

He led her out, and he himself looked absolutely drop-dead gorgeous in a frighteningly expensive black evening suit, cut to perfection on his broad shoulders, the black waistcoat fitting smoothly on his flat stomach and powerful chest, black trousers moulding his long, long muscular legs with sex appeal and authority as he walked, arrogant, handsome and very much in control.

Marie-Claire was waiting at the door in a slinky black evening dress.

'Oh, you look stunning!' Isabelle said, smiling.

'I know, *chérie*!' Marie-Claire laughed, twirling in her dramatic black. 'But you. . .you look more than stunning. You look absolutely breathtaking. You're going to knock the paparazzi for six.'

'Isn't she?' drawled Jean-Luc, sliding a possessive arm around Isabelle.

'Oh!' Madame Dusort appeared, half sobbing. 'You all look so wonderful! Have a lovely time and tell me what the Princesses wore!'

Jean-Luc laughed and they all said goodnight as he opened the front door and led them out, taking the lift down in a cloud of glamour and excitement to the foyer.

Of course, the Rolls took them along the coast, along the Avenue Princesse-Grace, along the richest strip of coastland in the whole Mediterranean. The Monte-Carlo Sporting Club was on a piece of rock jutting out beside the harbouresque setting of the Sea Club and close to Larvotto Beach, right on the coast of Monte-Carlo. A long procession of limousines, sports cars and more limousines glittered along the gold sunlit road towards it, crowds of people waiting to see the prince, the Prince Héréditaire, the princesses and all the film stars, supermodels, rock stars, personalities, multi-millionaires, fashion designers and glitterati arrive. As the white Rolls pulled up at the entrance, Jean-Luc got out and women started gasping, calling his name with excitement.

As if by magic, his face changed into the cool, dark, enigmatic lover of the public's perception. His dark brows seemed to arch satanically, the hooded lids drooped over his jet eyes, his tough face becoming more arrogant, dangerous and sexy by the second. He flicked a cool look at Isabelle, extended one strong hand, and helped her out.

A gasp went up around the crowds. The paparazzi swarmed *en masse* towards them as Jean-Luc led his red-haired, mysterious beauty to the doors of the world-famous Sporting Club.

'Who is she, Jean-Luc?'

The photographers' flashbulbs were blinding her.

'What's her name?'

He strode coolly past them, face arrogant, and did not reply.

Isabelle's hand slid through Jean-Luc's arm as she smiled at the cameras, green eyes flashing sexily through her lashes, swaying along beside him, keeping her head up, as excited as she was nervous, her long red-gold hair falling like silk against the glittering cream-gold fairy-tale dress.

The doors swung open. The doors swung shut. They were inside, and Isabelle felt breathless as she turned to him and said. 'Does that happen to you a lot?'

Jean-Luc looked at her with a hard smile and drawled, 'Yes, and you handled it beautifully, *chérie*. Well done.' He bent his dark head to kiss her cheek. 'I'm very proud of you.'

'Well!' laughed Marie-Claire behind them. 'I was quite overshadowed there! Oh! Hold on! Here comes a special car!'

They turned to see Princess Caroline stepping out of a black limousine.

'Isn't she beautiful?' sighed Marie-Claire.

Jean-Luc kissed Isabelle's hand. 'Come on, let's go and take our seats. I can see it's going to be an exceptional night.'

CHAPTER NINE

THE Salle des Etoiles of the Monte-Carlo Sporting
Club opened on to a sky illuminated by a thousand
lights, glittering and dazzling the eye in long rows
overhead, while mirrored glass and light pillars stood
along each wall. There were rows of long, long tables
laid with silver cutlery on rich linen, and each table
was filled with long rows of celebrities. Conversation
and laughter filled the vast *salle* as Jean-Luc, Isabelle
and Marie-Claire made their way to their seats, at a
table with some members of the prince's family, a
world-famous French fashion designer, and a handful
of people Isabelle had already met here in Monaco.
Waiters moved efficiently along the rows of star-
studded tables, pouring champagne.

'Jean-Luc, long time no see,' drawled a French film
star as they sat down a few seats from him. 'Who's the
beauty queen?'

'Ah, the beauty queen. . .' Jean-Luc murmured,
flicking his dark eyes to Isabelle, one powerful arm
resting behind her seat. 'That's you, Isabelle, isn't it?'

'I. . .' She faltered, wishing she could thank him,
deeply aware that he had done this for her, made her
beautiful again, given her back her self-confidence as
a woman, and brought her to the glittering occasion,
like a princess in her lovely dress. 'Yes, I suppose I
am. Thank you. . .' she found herself murmuring,
blushing as she lowered her lashes, eyes green with
confused emotion.

But why had he done it all for her? Just to get her

into bed with him? It was becoming traumatic to think about. Like a knife scratching the words 'He'll never love you' on to her heart.

Dinner was served a moment later, and Isabelle admired the exceptional dishes placed before her, but was quite unable to eat them. Jean-Luc displayed his usual non-existent appetite.

Conversation at the table was bright, brisk and superficially fun. They both talked to a number of people close by, to the film star, a blonde supermodel, a racing driver and a member of the princely family. Jean-Luc was treated with as much respect as always, and Isabelle knew she bathed in his popularity as everyone automatically included her in their conversation. The champagne made her heart ache even worse than ever, but she smiled and laughed and felt proud of Jean-Luc as he told a joke in that cool, sexy voice of his that made everyone roar with laughter and bang the table with their elegant hands.

Later, they sat back and finished the champagne, listening to the band as people began to dance, the lights lowered, and everything became bathed in a golden glow of champagne and relaxed enjoyment.

'Hey. . .beauty queen,' Jean-Luc murmured in her ear as he held her close, resting one long hand on the table. 'A franc for your thoughts.'

Her gaze flicked to his and she forced herself to say honestly, 'I—I was thinking about you. And why you've done all this for me.'

'I'll tell you later,' he drawled, 'when I'm making love to you.'

Her face paled. She looked away, moistening dry lips. 'I—I must just go to the powder-room. Can you tell me where it is?'

'Of course.' He gave her directions. 'But don't be

too long. I want to dance with you as soon as possible, then take you home to bed.' He kissed her mouth, a hard smile in his eyes. 'Off you go. . .'

Isabelle threaded her way through the long tables, smiling politely, and eventually found the powder-room, filled with beautiful women all gossiping and laughing and putting on lipstick, scent, touching up their hair with spray. Conversation stopped briefly as Isabelle appeared and they all stared at her, then started talking again.

Sinking down on a plush chair at the mirror, Isabelle pretended to repair her make-up. The truth was she needed to think.

'*J'ai envie de lui*!' one of the women drawled, putting on scarlet lipstick. 'And he fancies me, too. *Voilà*! Everything is *parfait*!'

'Lucky you,' said a blonde woman. 'I'm in love with Philippe, and he's always trying to get me into bed, but I know he doesn't love me, and he never will. What shall I do? I can't hold him off much longer!'

Isabelle's green eyes flicked to the blonde's reflection as her frantic mind picked up the parallel.

'Don't let him seduce you,' the brunette warned. 'It's always fatal. He'll just use you, then walk away.'

'But I love him so much,' the blonde said. 'I can't refuse him!'

Tell me about it, Isabelle thought bitterly, and her heart went out to the ravishing blonde in the sky-blue evening gown.

'We all have this problem, *chérie*, with our men,' said the brunette. 'And there is only one way to solve it. Either accept him as he is and let him make love to you — or leave him forever.'

She got to her feet, and moved away out of the room.

'That's Jean-Luc's latest!' The whispers began as she left.

'What a beauty! And that dress. . .'

'He'll drop her,' said scarlet lipstick. 'Once he's had her.'

Isabelle let the door slam, her face tight with fury and pain. She had to find a way to get away from him! Walking back to their table, she was thinking of ways of escape. Go to a hotel tonight? But how could she get away from Jean-Luc for long enough to get her passport and cheque-book, let alone pack her clothes?

As she got to her seat, she saw that Jean-Luc's seat was empty.

'Looking for Jean-Luc?' the French film star enquired. 'He's on the dance-floor with Louise Delavault.'

Isabelle felt sick suddenly, swaying, as jealousy and pain stabbed her so deep that she thought she might actually faint.

'Are you all right?' a voice said as long hands steadied her.

She spun with a frown to see Michel Balanchine. 'Oh. . .! Yes, I'm fine. Too much champagne, I think.'

'You need some fresh air.' He laughed. 'Let me take you outside and talk a while. Jean-Luc is dancing with his lovely friend, Loulou. He won't miss you.'

Isabelle shook her head, not wanting to let Jean-Luc know he had got the better of her, made her so appallingly jealous that she felt the need to run outside and hide from the sight of him dancing.

'Thank you,' she said politely, 'but I'm not that tipsy. I'll be fine. I just shouldn't have any more champagne.'

'Why not a dance, then?' he suggested brightly. 'If

Jean-Luc is smooching cheek-to-cheek with Loulou. . .?'

Her face flamed with humiliation. 'Yes, why not?' She lifted her bright head, green eyes flashing. 'Let's go and dance!'

He walked to the dance-floor with her, turning her into his arms as the band played a slow, sexy love song and all the couples were clinging glamorously in each other's arms.

'Mmm! You smell good!' Michel Balanchine said. 'Chanel No.5! Jean-Luc's favourite scent — did he buy it for you?'

Isabelle lowered her gaze, not wanting to answer that, angrily aware that the man already saw her as Jean-Luc's latest mistress.

She looked around for Jean-Luc and suddenly saw him on the other side of the dance-floor, the blonde Louise Delavault in his powerful arms as he danced cheek-to-cheek with her. Oh, the swine! Her veins boiled with savage jealousy and she jerked her gaze away, mouth trembling, tears stinging her eyes. How can he do it, when he knows what I've been through? How can he live with himself?

She saw it all now, so clearly, through a haze of pain.

Jean-Luc had deliberately set out to seduce her by making her fall in love with him. It had been his plan all along. And how easily he had achieved it, she thought bitterly, appalled at the brilliance of the invisible net he had thrown over her bit by bit until she was his, all his, just the latest fish he had caught with his unbelievable skill.

'What are you doing tomorrow night?' Michel murmured. 'I'd love to have dinner with you on my yacht. . .'

She barely heard, her heart in trauma. It had been deliberate. He had known she would fall in love with him. Why had she been such a fool as to believe he was only after her body? Surely she knew enough about him from his public image to know that he *never* just seduced women: he *always* made them fall in love with him, too.

'It's worth twenty million dollars,' Michel was saying somewhere above her bent head. 'Not as flashy as Jean-Luc's yacht, of course, but even so. . .'

Jean-Luc was dancing very close to Louise, his dark head bent to her slender throat, and his arms wrapped tightly around the blonde woman's slim body, elegant in a pale blue gown.

'I'm a very rich man. Not as rich as Jean-Luc, of course, but still worth mega-bucks. I have a private jet, too, if you ever want to fly to somewhere exotic with me. . .'

It was obvious that Jean-Luc was still carrying on an affair with Louise. Isabelle felt a fool for allowing herself to pretend blissfully that he might have told the truth when he said they were just friends. One more foolish, self-destructive move in a long line of self-destructive moves, she thought savagely.

'Did I tell you I know the President of the United States personally?' Michel Balanchine was now dropping names at a rate that almost eclipsed the one thousand lights in the Salle des Etoiles. 'I could introduce you to him, even take you to a White House ball. . .'

Oh, shut up, she thought, trying to keep her eyes on Jean-Luc, but he had disappeared in the last turn of the dance, and she was desperate to find him, terrified suddenly that he might be kissing Louise in a shadowy corner somewhere close by.

'My turn, I think!' Jean-Luc drawled bitingly above her head.

Isabelle spun with a gasp, staring up at him.

'No chance, Jean-Luc!' Michel said, holding on to Isabelle tightly. 'She's mine for the next three dances.'

'Not if you want to keep all your teeth,' Jean-Luc said pleasantly, and took Isabelle by the wrist.

'Hey!' Michel clung tightly to Isabelle. 'Hands off, Jean-Luc!'

There was a brief silence that bristled with aggression.

Jean-Luc's hand was hard on Isabelle's wrist. 'Let her go, Balanchine!'

'No.' He clung tight to her. 'And you're going to cause a scene if you try to fight me for her! Look — the paparazzi are taking pictures.'

Jean-Luc bit out under his breath, 'If it weren't for my respect for our prince and his family, I'd beat you to a pulp right here on the dance-floor. As it is, I refuse to embarrass them. I'm sure they've noticed you don't draw a similiar line on their behalf!'

Balanchine's eyes flickered uncertainly towards the tables.

'But next time I see you on the street——' Jean-Luc's eyes blazed with black violence as he towered over her other man '—I'm getting out of my car to give you the hiding of your miserable little life!'

'That's something you've wanted to do for a long time,' Balanchine shot back, but he was shaking even as he said it. 'You're not suddenly angry about this little fairy-tale redhead! You're still furious because I stole Hélène from you!'

Isabelle stared up at Jean-Luc, her tortured mind screaming, Hélène! Who is Hélène?

'You were welcome to that mercenary little bitch!'

Jean-Luc bit out thickly. 'But you're not getting your hands on Isabelle, and if you don't let her go immediately, Balanchine, I'll have you run out of this principality so fast you won't know what's hit you! Now let her go!'

Balanchine stepped back at once, his face white.

Jean-Luc turned on his heel, his face white with rage, and pulled Isabelle after him, stopping at the table.

'Get your bag, we're leaving.'

'But it's only eleven ——'

'I said we're leaving!' he bit out forcefully and the look on his face brooked no argument whatsoever.

Pale, she reached for her bag, murmured polite goodbyes to the now half-empty table, and a few minutes later they were walking out into the hot dark night where the paparazzi photographed them as they walked quickly to the white Rolls, got into it and Jean-Luc bit out to the chauffeur, 'Get us home, fast!'

They drove away with a squeal of tyres while the flashbulbs were still exploding.

'Why did you dance with him?' Jean-Luc bit out thickly as the car sped on to the Avenue Princesse-Grace. 'After I specifically demanded that you never, ever speak to him again, I turn round the very next night and find you smooching on the dance-floor with him!' His voice had risen in fury, his eyes leaping with rage. 'At the Red Cross Ball! With all of Monaco watching and half the world's Press! They got everything! Those pictures they took on the dance-floor will tell the whole story!'

He lunged at her, catching her shoulders in a furious grip. 'How could you do that to me?'

'You were dancing with Louise!' she broke out in fierce jealous pain. 'And you were the ones who were smooching! I thought you were going to kiss her, right there, in front of me!'

'So you decided to dance with him to get your own back on me!'

'No! It never even occurred to me that you'd notice us!'

His eyes blazed as the breeze flicked his black hair back. 'Of course I noticed you! I've spent the whole time since you arrived noticing everything you do! Why should I suddenly stop tonight?'

'Because you were dancing with your other mistress!'

His teeth met. 'I'm not even going to discuss that with you! You deliberately danced with Balanchine to stab me in the back, publicly! And, my God, I'm going to teach you a lesson for it! I'm going to teach you never, ever, *ever* to mess with me like that again!'

'Don't pretend it's me you're angry with! Don't pretend you were jealous or hurt because I danced with another man!' Her eyes blazed with fury. 'It's Michel Balanchine you're angry with! I heard what he said about that woman! What was her name again? Hélène? Is that —— ?'

'Shut up!' he bit out thickly.

The car pulled up outside the apartment block. Jean-Luc took her by the wrist, dragging her furiously into the foyer, pushing her into the lift and jabbing the button for the *dernier étage*.

'Well?' she asked bitterly, hating him. 'It's Hélène that upsets you, isn't it? Hélène and Balanchine!'

'I told you to shut up!' he bit out as the lift rode up.

'He stole her away from you, didn't he?' Her voice shook. 'And you loved her! You were in love with a woman called Hélène, whom Balanchine stole from you, and your rage tonight has everything to do with her — and nothing to do with me!'

'You don't seriously think I'm going to discuss Hélène with you?'

She flinched as though he'd slapped her hard across the face.

'I wouldn't tell you the colour of the moon now,' he bit out icily. 'You're history as far as I'm concerned.'

Isabelle gave a grunt of pain, turning her face away, mouth shaking. 'Good. . . I'm glad I'm history! That means I can leave this apartment tonight and get away from you forever!'

'Oh, no, you can't!' he said though his teeth. 'I've invested too much time and energy in you, and I'm going to have you.'

The lift doors opened. Isabelle looked at him with sudden horror.

'Come on.' His hand bit into her wrist, face ruthless as he pulled her out and across the hallway though she struggled. 'It's bedtime with all the trimmings!'

Breathless, appalled, she fought him. 'Stop it. . .no. . .!'

'You've been driving me crazy ever since I first saw you! I've wanted to make love to you, thought about it obsessively, tried to help you, played a waiting game, spent every second biting my knuckles and struggling to keep my hands off you! But I've been too patient with you, much too patient. I thought tonight would be —— ' His mouth tightened as he looked down at her, eyes bitter. 'At any rate, it's time you gave me some kind of satisfaction. I don't see why I should carry on being patient with you any longer!'

'You haven't been patient!' she said fiercely. 'You've pushed and forced your way into my life without invitation of any kind!'

His lip curled in a sneer. 'Oh, I had plenty of invitation, *chérie*!'

Isabelle slapped his face, a hoarse cry of pain in her throat as her hand stung him across the cheek. He smiled angrily, took her by the wrists, dragged her into the apartment and up the corridor while she kicked and cried out in growing desperation.

He kicked open his bedroom door, whirled her in. 'Get inside and give me what I've been working for!'

She stumbled in, breathing hard. 'If you touch me, I swear I'll scream the place down!'

'Go ahead,' he drawled, tearing his bow-tie off and throwing it to the floor, advancing on her. 'The last screams you give will be of intense satisfaction. I can't wait to hear them.'

She backed, her heart banging violently. 'Get away from me, Jean-Luc, I mean every word I say!'

'So do I, *chérie*!' He shouldered out of his evening jacket, threw it to the floor. 'I wanted our first night together in bed to be a beautiful, sensual dream. But you evidently prefer to behave like a whore, so I'll treat you like one. Now, get on the bed.'

'Why are you doing this?' she whispered hoarsely. 'Why are you being so vicious?'

He studied her, and suddenly his mouth shook as he said hoarsely, 'Because I know what was really going on in your mind when you were dancing with Balanchine tonight! You said you were going to try and find a new man, didn't you? Last night you said it, and I didn't believe you, but I do now!' Pain blazed in his dark eyes. 'I made it more than clear how badly I'd react if you ever spoke to Balanchine again. But that's why you decided to pick him, isn't It? To stick a knife in me and——'

'I only danced with him!'

'Cheek-to-cheek!' He was striding over to her, his voice shaking with emotion. 'Well, you can run off with him with my blessings! But I'll have you first. I'll have you and then I'll throw you out of the apartment first thing tomorrow morning.'

'No! Oh, my God, how can you do this?'

'Because you've pushed me to it!' His hands gripped her shoulders; he was breathing harshly, his skin tautly stretched over hard bones. 'Get out of that pretty dress, *chérie*! The fairy-tale is over!'

'No!' Pain made her voice raw. 'You'll have to tear it from me!'

'Why not?' he said thickly. 'You've torn my dreams to shreds!' His hands caught the silk, ready to rip it.

'No, I won't let you!' Her hand stung him viciously across the face, making his head jerk back, eyes blazing with rage.

'That's it!' he bit out hoarsely. 'I've had quite enough of you for one lifetime!' He caught her by the shoulders and threw her back, then followed her, eyes blazing.

She landed on the bed. 'No!' She scrambled frantically away from him, white and shaking. 'No, I won't let you do it, I won't let you!'

She screamed as his hard mouth closed over hers, pushing her lips apart punishingly, wanting to hurt her, bruising her lips as she fought him bitterly, raining fierce blows on his face, his shoulders, his chest.

'Lie still!' He thrust her legs apart with one angry thigh.

'No, get off me!' She was writhing and bucking under his powerful body, her hands like a windmill as she hit him in deadly earnest.

'I said lie still!' he bit out hoarsely, struggling to undo her zip.

Isabelle slapped him so hard around the face that he jerked back for just long enough for her to scramble off the bed and run frantically for the bedroom door.

'Come back here!' Jean-Luc leapt up, red in the face with rage as he sprinted after her, eyes blazing, voice raw. 'I'll kill you, you —— '

'Go ahead!' she cried hoarsely, flinching against the door. 'My husband would be proud of you! I bet he's cheering in hell right now!'

He stopped dead, breathing hard, staring down at her, then bit out an obscenity in French and turned on his heel, striding away from her, thrusting his hands in his black trouser pockets, standing by the closed doors of his balcony windows, breathing thickly.

She gradually straightened, shaking from head to foot, tears stinging her eyes.

'All right, I'm not going to rape you!' Jean-Luc said thickly, his back to her. 'But stay away from me until you've found somewhere else to go. And find it fast. I want you out before I get back from work tomorrow night. I never want to set eyes on you again!' His voice shook. 'Go on, get out of my sight!'

'I'm going!' she whispered, tears blurring her vision. 'But before I go, I just want to tell you what a terrible thing you've done to me, and how deeply you've added to the damage since I met you!'

'I'm not interested!' he said shakily. 'Just get out of my sight and stay out of it!'

'You said you'd break my heart and I should have believed you. It was deliberate, wasn't it? You didn't just want to get me into bed. You wanted to make me fall in love with you, and you have.'

He spun, staring, his face white.

'You got what you wanted.' Tears slipped over her lashes. 'I'm in love with you. I hope you're satisfied!'

She wrenched open the door and ran, blind as the tears fell burningly over her lashes.

'No!' Jean-Luc bit out thickly as she ran from the room. 'No. . .!'

But she was already blindly wrenching the front door open and running for the lift, pressing the button to find it still there, doors sliding open so that she could run in and jab fiercely at the ground-floor button.

'Isabelle, wait!' Jean-Luc ran out into the hall.

The lift doors slid shut. She was going down, her hands covering her tear-stained face. She shouldn't have told him. Did she have no pride? But she had been so hurt, so angry, so devastated by his behaviour and the vicious, wicked things he had said to her. She had wanted to throw something at him to make him feel ashamed, but now she could see he would only use it to his own advantage.

Of course he came running after me, she thought, sobbing hoarsely. He knows he can use my love as a weapon to manipulate me into bed with him. He'll probably tell me he loves me too, she thought with horror.

The lift arrived at the ground floor. Isabelle ran out of it, out on to the streets, her ballgown glittering as she ran along the Avenue de la Madone without thinking, tears streaming down her face, crying so hard she thought her heart must have cracked clean across.

Shop windows flew by in a haze, a car drove slowly past, and she didn't even stop to consider how she must look, a woman in a ballgown running crying through the streets.

'Isabelle!' Jean-Luc shot out of the apartment building like a bullet from a gun, shouting hoarsely after her in the dark street. 'Wait!'

He's going to tell me he loves me, she thought in

despair, talk me into going back to the apartment, and seduce me. She kept running, the hem of the ballgown dusty and frayed now, her breath coming faster, her heart banging hard and the tears rolling hotly down her cheeks.

Suddenly, she was in the square as the glowing clock struck midnight on the Monte-Carlo casino, and she stared up at it, tears blurring her vision, seeing the stone angels guarding the block, the palm trees towering high as the sculpted turrets of that baroque stone palace.

'Isabelle, come back. . .!' Jean-Luc was catching up with her.

Panic-stricken, she ran towards the light, towards the casino, towards the gleaming art nouveau carriage-lamps and the three great oak-glass doors of the sanctuary it now represented to her.

There would be people there, hundreds of wealthy gamblers, cars driving up, paparazzi waiting to take photographs. He would not follow her if she went there.

'Stop!' He caught her as she ran across the gardens, past the fountain, the illuminated water spraying in a silvery arc beside the palm trees and flowers.

'Let me go!' She tried to pull away.

'No!' He was dragging air into his lungs. 'I have to talk to you; I didn't know you loved me, I——'

'Don't you try to use what I told you in a moment of weakness! That won't get me into bed with you!' She hit out at him and ran across the gardens, past the fountain, on to the street in front of the casino.

His hand caught her wrist again. 'No, wait! You don't understand what I'm trying to say! I'm in love with you, too! Isabelle, forgive me, please! Come home with me and——'

She lashed out at him in blind fury and ran again, tears blurring her eyes.

'Listen to me!' He caught her at the foot of the steps. 'I was going to propose when we got home from the ball. I had the ring—it was in my jacket; I had it with me all night, I——'

'No!' She sobbed, shaking her head fiercely. 'No, I can't believe you. . .I mustn't. . .'

'It's true.' His voice was shaking. 'I love you, *chérie*; please come home and let me——'

'No!' Fear made her push at him and run up the steps, desperate to get away before he convinced her that he really meant it then got his revenge by taking her to bed and throwing her out in the morning.

'You must believe me!' he shouted, running up the steps to stop her. 'Come home and see the ring! It's still in my jacket, in the bedroom——'

'I'm never going back to that apartment again!' she said fiercely. 'I'm leaving Monaco tomorrow; you can send my things on to——'

'No!' He went white. 'I won't let you leave me!'

'You can't stop me!'

They were on the steps of the casino.

'I love you!' He went down on one knee, his hand gripping hers. 'Will you marry me?'

A flashbulb exploded as the crowd gasped.

She couldn't breathe, just stood there, staring down at him.

'My whole future is now in your hands!' he told her. 'Don't destroy me, please marry me, say yes!'

'Yes!' she whispered.

He got to his feet, pulling her into his arms, his mouth closing over hers in a deep, fierce kiss as the flashbulb exploded again and again and he crushed her slender body against his.

CHAPTER TEN

'I LOVE you, I love you,' Isabelle whispered against his hot mouth.

'Isabelle!' he breathed thickly. 'I thought you'd never believe me!'

'I was so afraid, so convinced you wanted nothing but sex. . .'

'I had to make you think that. It was the only explanation I could give for my behaviour.' He gave an unsteady laugh, kissing her cheek. 'I couldn't leave you alone for five seconds! My God, even Marie-Claire knew I was head over heels in love! Taking time off work, cornering you endlessly, buying you that absurdly romantic ballgown!'

'She knew?' Isabelle was breathless. 'You mean you told her?'

'Of course I didn't! Wild horses couldn't have dragged it out of me! But she's my sister and she knows me, *chérie*. You must have noticed all her cryptic little comments about us? Calling us lovebirds, saying we couldn't leave each other alone, making herself scarce all the time.'

'I thought it was because she didn't want to interfere with your skilled seduction of me,' she confessed.

He laughed and shook his dark head. '*Chérie*, you're always talking about my skill, but you must see that with that skill and experience I could have taken you any time I wanted. Particularly when you were model-ling that lingerie for me. Had I wanted nothing from you but sex, that is precisely when I would have got it.' He smiled at her, murmuring softly, 'Now come home with me, *ma chère*. I want that ring on your finger before you ever get the chance to run away from me again!'

They turned, hand in hand, and walked down the steps as the small crowd began to disperse, chauffeurs leaning on their employers' Rolls-Royces smiling indulgently while tourists hung back by the trees.

The lone paparazzi took another shot of them. 'Thanks, Jean-Luc! Those pictures will earn me a bloody fortune!' He was backing away, grinning. 'I owe you one!'

'Clear off, André!' Jean-Luc said flatly. 'Just because I'm in a good mood, it doesn't mean I won't punch your face in and steal your film!'

'You'd have to catch me first!' André shot away to a motorbike and revved the engine, roaring away a second later.

'I don't believe it,' Jean-Luc bit out with a dry laugh. 'The most important private moment of my life, and the paparazzi get it, frame by frame, on film.'

Isabelle frowned. 'I'm sorry. That was my fault. But I ran to the casino because I was so sure it was the one place you wouldn't follow.'

He grimaced, slid an arm around her and started walking home, drawling coolly, 'It must be fate. I can't change it. But when I think what they've got tonight! Oh, God. . .' He laughed under his breath as he walked with her out of the casino square. 'Us arriving at the ball, then the row on the dance-floor, and finally — the *pièce de résistance* — me proposing to you! Down on one knee, on the casino steps! It's at least a ten-page spread with accompanying drivel! I hate them! Off with their heads!'

Isabelle looked up at him, uncertain suddenly. 'You

could always say it was just a publicity stunt. You don't have to marry me if you ——'

'*Chérie*,' he said, 'when will you recognise how deeply I am in love with you, and have been since the moment I first saw you?'

Her lips parted in shock. 'What. . .? Since you first saw me?'

'Oh, did I forget to tell you?' he drawled softly, walking along Avenue de la Madone with her. 'Yes, it was when I got out of my car at Nice airport. I looked at you and felt myself suddenly drop flat on my knees. Then I realised I was still standing up straight, and I was so amazed I took my sunglasses off to stare at you in case I'd imagined you.'

'But. . .' her heart was beating wildly with love '. . .but I had no idea! I thought you were just staring out of sexual interest!'

He laughed. 'Well, I could hardly tell you the truth, could I? Especially when you were looking at me so contemptuously. Then, when I tried to charm you, you just kept rejecting me. I was devastated by the time we landed at Fontvielle. I couldn't see any way to turn the situation around. Then I caught you looking at me in the rear-view mirror.'

'And guessed how I really felt under my hatred!' she groaned.

'Oh, yes,' he murmured, 'and what a lucky realisation that was! I suddenly thought, Hang on a minute! She snaps at you continually, says you make all her hackles rise, and stares at you when you're not looking. . .she fancies you, you idiot! Get her alone and make her admit it!'

Isabelle laughed, blushing pink. 'I was so terrified when you refused to accept my apology that day. I could barely think straight.'

'I know, and that's when I had my first inkling that all was not well with your confidence as a woman. You quite obviously didn't understand what I was trying to make you admit. You didn't even know you fancied me. In a seventeen-year-old, that would be acceptable. But a woman of twenty-six with a marriage behind her and three years living in a foreign continent? No. It didn't add up. That's why I came to your bedroom after an hour. I knew the only way to make you admit it was to kiss you.'

'You'll never know how shocked I was. I couldn't believe it when you started walking across the room towards me with that look in your eyes.'

'I was thinking on my feet,' he drawled. 'I'd intended to give you a very thorough kissing, but I didn't realise quite how frightened you'd be when I tried. That's why I just grabbed you and got it over with. I knew it was the only way to get the ball rolling. Left up to you, we'd have just lived in a sexual and emotional battlefield forever.'

'Oh, absolutely,' she said, dismayed at the thought of how easily that could have happened. 'I remember when you said that in the car park, too. That you weren't prepared to live like that. I had no idea what was happening between us, but I did begin to realise how determined you were then, and how quick to leap on any little clue I gave you.'

'I was head over heels in love, *chérie*.' They reached the apartment and went into the foyer. 'I couldn't think of anything but you. It really was a *coup de foudre*. I was hit by lightning. Abracadabra.'

Isabelle kissed his handsome cheek. 'I think I was, too, but it took me a lot longer to recognise it.'

'Yes. . .' He stepped into the lift with her, a cool smile on his tough mouth. 'And when exactly did you

recognise it? When did you know you were in love
with me?'

'Last night,' she admitted huskily. 'Although I knew
I was in danger before that. It was as gradual a process,
Jean-Luc, as admitting that I wanted to make love
with you. It was there immediately, but I was too
scared and too badly damaged to be able to admit it.'

He studied her with those dark eyes. 'You've been
through hell, *ma chère*, haven't you? But I have a little
confession to make. So have I. My rage when you
spoke to Balanchine has a powerful trauma behind it.'

Isabelle looked at him with a sudden pang of jealous
fear. 'Hélène. . .?'

'No need to look jealous, *chérie*,' he said softly,
leading her out of the lift and across the hallway to the
front doors of the apartment. 'In many ways, Hélène
was my version of Anthony. She was a beautiful
model, I was thirty-one, and in a moment of arrogant
conceit that changed my life forever I decided she
would be a good showpiece wife.'

'You've been married too,' she said, amazed, as he
opened the appartment doors.

'No, I didn't marry her, thank God.' He shuddered,
threw his keys on the hall table and walked towards
the bedroom corridor with her. 'But I did get engaged
to her, publicly, complete with colour spreads in
magazines and declarations of love.'

'What happened?' she asked, deciding not to notice
the fact that he was taking her into his bedroom and
closing the door behind them.

'Hélène was as egotistical and wrapped up in her
own self-image as I was. I'd decided to marry her
because she suited my public image. When she realised
I wasn't remotely in love with her. . .well, you know
what they say: hell hath no fury like a woman scorned.

And Hélène really took me by the throat and taught me what that phrase can mean. She went out of her way to nail me up against the wall, to destroy my public image by running off with Michel Balanchine and flaunting her rejection of me at every possible opportunity.'

Isabelle sank on to the bed, listening. 'What did you do?'

'Nothing,' he drawled, sitting down beside her with a sardonic smile. 'Absolutely nothing. I couldn't afford to react publicly. I knew that immediately. The first hint of any emotional reaction from me would have given her her revenge and undoubtedly humiliated me to within an inch of my life in the international Press. Think of it, *chérie*. Think of what they got tonight, from us, when we were genuinely in love. And think of what they could have got from me five years ago with Hélène and Balanchine.' He studied her, dark brows arching. 'Imagine. . .photos of me punching Balanchine in a fit of rage. Photos of me shouting angrily at Hélène. Photos of me storming out of nightclubs where they were on the dance-floor, right in front of my face, French kissing and giving me mocking looks.' He paused, seeing the horror in her eyes as she found herself able to picture it very clearly. 'No. My only possible escape was to do nothing at all, just get on with my own life and ensure that not a single drop of their poison tainted my public image.'

Isabelle looked into his dark eyes. 'But inside. . .?'

'Ah. . .' He took her hand in his. 'Inside, *chérie*, I was devastated. I couldn't begin to handle such humiliation. My only refuge was here, in this apartment, and as the agonising weeks wore on I began to split away from the outside world, tearing myself away from my public image and finding that it was a shallow, ugly, empty way of life that I could no longer tolerate. Yet I had no choice. I had built it in my arrogant youth, and it was nailed very firmly on to me. The Press, I gradually realised, would leap at the chance to give me a very different image, if I allowed them to. The image of a reformed millionaire playboy who got kicked in the teeth for his own conceit and never recovered. But you will agree, *ma chère*, that that was not the course for me to take.'

'Jean-Luc. . . I had no idea you'd suffered like this.'

He smiled. 'No. You see how well I maintained my dignity.'

'It's incredible,' she said in breathless admiration. 'Nobody could possibly guess. Certainly I didn't. I believed every word of your image, every article I ever read, every photograph I ever saw. That's why when I met you I was so convinced you wanted only to seduce me.'

'Hmm.' The dark eyes glinted. 'Well, I did and still do want to seduce you, *chérie*. But I must tell you I haven't played that way with women for five years. That's why I spend so much time at work. Of course, there have been women since then, but very few, and always very carefully selected. I wasn't damaged as badly as you, Isabelle, because I managed to stop people finding out what had happened inside me. But I was damaged. For the better, I think. Certainly. . .falling head over heels in love with a beautiful, like-minded redhead called Isabelle has suddenly made everything worthwhile.'

'*Chéri*!' She put her arms around his strong neck, kissing him. 'I loved you before you told me that, but I have to admit I felt my love deepening with every word you said! My God, how it all makes sense! No wonder you were so patient with me, so gentle, always knowing exactly how to handle my emotions at every step. You'd been through it all yourself!'

'And fell more deeply in love with you with every word you told me,' he said huskily, 'that night I made you confess everything. It was so moving, *chérie*. That's why I didn't dare stop and reassure you whenever you started running yourself down, saying how hopeless you were. I knew I had to get everything out of you if I was to help you recover. It had taken very serious threats from me to make you talk in the first place. I couldn't run the risk of you clamming up. Besides, I knew the only way to give you back your sexual confidence was in practice; not theory.'

She blushed, smiling at him through her lashes, whispering, 'Oh, your presents. . .'

'I loved choosing them,' he said softly. 'And when I came home to find you laughing softly as you played with them on the bed. . .ah, *chérie*! I was so moved, and so very excited. I was frightened by how much I wanted to make love to you. I lost control at the end, tearing off my tie and dragging air into my lungs. And that, I can assure you, is so unprecedented as to be staggering.' His dark eyes glinted as he drawled softly, 'I may have changed emotionally, but I am still the very skilled and experienced lover I became famous as. And I, let me tell you, have never lost control with a woman.'

She laughed softly and her fingers slid to the top button of his shirt. His face changed as he drew a sharp breath, eyes darkening to black fire. 'Ah. . .don't tempt me now, *chérie*.'

Isabelle looked at him hotly through her lashes. 'I loved your presents. . .do you want to see what I'm wearing under this gown?'

His heart began to thud heavily at his chest as his breath came faster and his gaze lowered to her body.

Slowly, watching him, she put trembling hands to her back and began to slide down the zip of her dress as dark colour flooded his face and he remained where he was, very still, staring at her. The dress fell softly from her shoulders, revealing her full breasts, and her heart was pounding with terrible excitement as she slowly slid it over her hips, shaking with half-renewed confidence as she let it fall softly to the floor to reveal her lacy briefs and soft, silky stockinged thighs.

Breathing shakily, she put trembling hands on his shoulders and knelt beside him on the bed, whispering, '*Chéri*, I'm in your hands, tell me what to do. . .!'

'Just stay in my hands, and let me do it all!' he said thickly, and then his hot mouth closed over hers in a long, slow, sexy kiss.

He slid her gently back on to the bed with him. He turned her in his arms so that she lay beneath him. His mouth moved sensually, commandingly over hers, making her dizzy and breathless, fingers shaking on his shoulders, heart thumping madly, her whole body responding like wildfire to his touch, his kiss, his hard thighs against hers as he sprawled slowly across her and reached out one strong hand to punch off the main light, flick on the lamp, dimming the lighting to an intimate glow.

Delirious, she was moving softly against him, her eyes closed and her body alive with pulses. As she felt his hard thigh slowly part hers, she moaned, and a moment later his hot mouth was closing over her burning nipple, sucking it skilfully as she gasped beneath him, her hands in his dark hair, whispering his name, whispering it over and over again as he took absolute mastery of her shaking, burning body.

Her mouth was hot, swollen with passion as they kissed deeply, and she could feel him unbuttoning his waistcoat, heard it fall to the floor, heard the soft thud of his shoes as he slowly kicked them off, kissing her all the time, before his long fingers began to unbutton his white shirt.

'*Caresse moi*,' he murmured shakily against her mouth as he dropped his shirt to the floor, and she ran her hands over that hard, hot chest with growing excitement, feeling the rapid thud of his heart.

He was sliding long fingers to her thighs. She started to moan deliriously in anticipation, and as he slowly stroked the soft, scented skin of her inner thighs she began to pulse hotly against him, her body rocking gently as she spread her legs in natural invitation.

Jean-Luc gave a hoarse groan and his mouth deepened the kiss, heat burning between them now as his hand moved to stroke her lacy briefs down, slowly, very slowly, sliding them over her slim hips while she moaned beneath him, gasping against his tongue, desire surging through her in terrifying intensity.

She was naked suddenly—or was it slowly?—twisting against his firm hands as they slid up her thighs, spread them slowly, his fingers moving upwards, upwards, until they stroked the hot, slippery centre of her femininity where no one had touched her for three years.

'Ah, *chérie*. . .' He was breathing hoarsely, his heart banging hard, his long finger sliding slowly inside her as she pulsed in wanton, breathless pleasure beneath him. 'Oh, God. . .! *Ah, je te veux*!' He dragged air into his lungs, groaning as his hands fumbled with the zip of his trousers, his face burning dark red, eyes like black fire. '*Je t'aime! Je suis le tien*!'

Isabelle's breathing was hoarse, ragged, coming

thicker and faster as he pushed his clothes off, coming back to her naked, and the hard throbbing jut of his rigid manhood against her hot, moist, open flesh made her cry out in agonised excitement.

'Take me, take me!' she whispered in hoarse need, clinging to his bare shoulders, her body open, hot, pulsing against his.

He pushed inside her, spreading her wide, and shuddered in delicious pleasure as she gave a long, shaking cry of intense satisfaction, her arms going round him, the feel of naked skin locking with naked skin making her scalp prickle with unbearable excitement and her body gasp air into her lungs, almost sobbing now, shaking from head to foot.

'Don't move, *chérie*!' he said hoarsely against the throbbing pulse in her throat. 'Let me show you the way. . .' His long fingers slid to the slippery bud of flesh between her thighs, and he kissed her deeply as he stroked it, whispering thickly in wicked French to her, telling her how much he loved her, wanted her, all the delicious, sensual things he wanted to do to her, and asking her again and again, 'Yes? Is that what you need? Yes? You'd like me to do it? Yes? Yes. . .?'

'Yes. . .!' she screamed in sudden agonised release as she was flung into ecstasy like a bullet from a gun, hurtling into dark pleasure, and her body jerked in uncontrollable spasms, hot and wet and violently delicious, every muscle gripped and shaken with a pleasure so intense she thought she'd black out. But gradually it began to subside into a steady roll of delicous hot spasms, coming slow but sure as she lay back with her eyes shut and her mouth open, moaning softly until she rocked to an exhausted standstill of absolute sexual satisfaction and opened her eyes, sweat on her lashes, gasping for breath.

He stared down at her, shaking. '*Oh, chérie*. . .' he said hoarsely, dragging air into his lungs as his hands tightened on her hips.

With a long, fierce groan he started to drive into her for his own satisfaction, his teeth suddenly clamping together as he pummelled her with his body, breathing as though he were about to die, his eyes on fire and his face so darkly flushed it was burning up.

He gave a shout of disbelief and the breath was punched violently out of him. He stilled within her, rigid, shuddering, his eyes tightly shut and his throat making incoherent strangled noises. Then he gasped, his body jerking back, then slamming into her again, shaking from head to foot as he cried out in agonised pleasure, his heartbeat so violent it seemed to bang throughout the room like a fierce drum.

He collapsed against her breast. 'I thought I'd black out!' he said hoarsely. 'I really did. I thought, This is it. You're going to just lose consciousness and there's nothing you can do about it.' He closed his eyes on a rough groan. 'Oh, my God, Isabelle! I've never felt anything so intense. I'm so much in love with you. . .'

'I've never felt anything like it,' she whispered, tears in her eyes, 'intense or otherwise. Jean-Luc, I—I don't know how to tell you this, but I——'

'I know,' he said softly, raising his head, still struggling to breathe even as he smiled down at her. 'Do you really think you needed to tell me that you'd never experienced orgasm before?'

Her face burnt and she lowered her lashes, saying shakily, 'I—I feel so inadequate!'

'Oh, no.' He kissed her deeply. 'No, *chérie*. How can you be inadequate when you make a man of my experience almost black out with pleasure? Hmm?' He smiled, eyes filled with love. '*Chérie*, you're quite the most exciting lover. Your responses are so natural, so relaxed and rich with pulsing sensuality.' He laughed softly under his breath, drawling, 'You're a natural. And the fact that it's only ever going to be like this with me just makes me feel ill with pleasure.'

'Well. . .' She believed him, but she was tentative still, saying, 'Why did it take me so long, then? To — to reach this point as a woman?'

'That's simple,' he said gently. 'You were mildly repressed when you married Anthony. I expect it was all that Southern refinement, being a lady and having to maintain a very ladylike image in every walk of life. But sexuality and ladylike behaviour do not make good bedfellows. In fact, they're totally opposed to each other. So when you married Anthony and found yourself in bed with a man you neither loved nor wanted sexually, you were in trouble. And Anthony, though I hate to speak ill of the dead, quite obviously didn't know the first thing above love, women or sex.'

She listened, her confidence growing. 'Do you think that's why I eventually started tearing your clothes off? Because I really was walking around on the edge of explosion, and didn't realise it until you forced me to admit I wanted you?'

'I think that's a very good description,' he drawled, laughing. 'And admitting the truth is always the most important part of any process in life. After all, if we look at it on a purely businesslike level, what would be the point of my studying an account book and telling myself that the total was, say, fifty million instead of two hundred million?'

She gasped, staring, goggle-eyed. 'How much?'

He laughed, and kissed her nose. 'I forget! Besides, it was merely an example. You don't get anywhere unless the truth is faced and dealt with. And that goes for love as well as business.'

'That's why you were so brutal sometimes with me,' she realised slowly. 'I used to hate you so much for it. Finding the scars and pressing them one by one. It was agony.'

'They were thorns, *chérie*, and I have extracted every last one of them. You are now my lover, my fiancée and soon to be my wife. Ah! That reminds me! The ring is still in my jacket. Where is that?'

'Give it to me later,' she said with a smile. 'It was the declaration of love that was important to me.'

He smiled. 'It's a very big emerald, *chérie*. . .and it will look wonderful on your finger when we fly into New Orleans in my private jet for your first visit home in three years.'

'Oh. . .!' Her eyes shone with sudden delight. 'Oh, yes. . . I can go home now! See my parents, see my old friends, see New Orleans again!'

'But in style, *chérie*,' he warned with a lift of dark brows. 'You and I know you are rebuilt, but the town must be shown that, too. And I'll enjoy seeing to it for you. I think a twenty-foot white Cadillac is a good idea, and a dazzling wardrobe for all the publicity I shall quite deliberately stir up on our arrival.'

Isabelle laughed and bit her lip. 'You're very naughty!'

'I know!' His dark eyes glinted. 'But this you must do. You have learned the hard way that reputation is very important. You're going to be marrying an expert in the art, and——' He laughed suddenly, and shook his head. 'An expert! When I think of what they got tonight! Oh, no. . .!' He buried his face in her neck. 'All those pictures! I can't bear it! I thought I had it all sewn up; it's the first slip I've made in five years, and

what a slip! Proposing on the steps of the casino!
They'll have every inch of love written all over my face
in horrible close-up!'

'You could give an interview saying——'

'No way on God's earth!' He lifted his head, frowning. 'No! I never give interviews, never. Only to
business magazines, serious newspapers, and people
asking me about my work. The pop papers and glossy
gossip magazines get nothing from me. Just a cool
click at the end of the telephone if they manage to get
hold of my private number.'

She smiled. 'I'm glad to hear you say that, actually.
I don't think I'd like to live in a goldfish bowl.'

'You don't have to in Monaco, *chérie*. The paparazzi
are surrounded by celebrities, day and night. This
place is jam-packed with them. It's true being photographed is a way of life here, but at least they don't
bother to chase or stalk you unless something big is
happening. Most of the time, celebrities in Monaco
are free to do as they please.'

'Monaco. . .' she said softly, eyes glowing. 'You
know, I always felt drawn here, ever since I was very
young, listening to my father telling me about the
magical little principality by the sea, and the beautiful
princes and princesses who lived there in a fairy-tale
castle.'

He smiled. 'You'll live here with me for the rest of
your life, my darling, and our children will be
Monégasque because I am, and nationality passes
through the male here.'

Her lashes flickered, wonder in her stricken face.
'Children. . .oh, Jean-Luc, yes, please! I—I wanted to
have children so much, but I always thought it was
impossible because of what had happened to me. I
thought I'd never fall in love, never love and be loved,

never have the chance to even start considering children!'

He kissed her deeply. 'All that's over, *chérie*. It's in the past now. You came to Monaco and transformed into what you really were all along—a very beautiful, charming, sensual and intelligent woman with a wonderful capacity for love and a great future.'

'You transformed me. And I love you so much I can't even begin to tell you what you mean to me. I feel as though something exceptional has happened to me—as though I've stepped into a fairy-tale!'

'*Chérie*,' he drawled softly, 'you are in Monaco, where the exceptional is a way of life, and fairy-tales are the stuff of which our history is made. . .'

And as he bent his head to kiss her she knew her childhood dreams had not been dreams at all, for here she was, beautiful and loved and being kissed by her handsome prince.

Welcome to Europe

MONACO — 'the heart of glamour'

Monaco is a place to dress up, have fun and spend money! Tucked away into the coast of southern France, between Nice and the Italian border, curving in a U-shape around the little headland jutting into an aquamarine sea, the tiny principality known as a tax haven and luxury gambling centre spells romance for the jet set and offers a little slice of *la dolce vita* for those who are simply passing through.

THE ROMANTIC PAST

Monaco town was known to the Romans as **Portus Monoeci** or Port Hercules, but it was of little use to them then except as a shelter in a storm, for it lacked any habitable hinterland except for steep cliffs and mountains.

It became an independent lordship in 1308, when the first of the **Grimaldi** family acquired it from the Genoese, and it has remained in that family ever since, though sometimes passing through the female line (their husbands chose to take on the Grimaldi name, unsurprisingly!). Legend has it that the first Grimaldi entered the impregnable castle disguised as a monk, which is why monks and a sword appear on the Grimaldi shield today.

During the nineteenth century, when the provinces of Menton and Roquebrune were lost, and with them a main source of income from oil and lemons, the therefore impoverished principality decided to turn itself into a gambling haven, gambling being at that time forbidden by law in France. Its first attempt failed dismally because of poor communications, and Prince Charles III brought in a French 'whiz-kid' to set up a new resort, known ever since as the *Société des Bains de Mer* — the Sea-bathing Society. This, combined with the opening in 1868 of the railway from Nice, ensured Monaco's fortunes as a glamorous resort. In winter 1887, for example, the Hôtel de Paris had among its illustrious guests the King of Sweden, the Queen of Portugal, the Dowager Empress of Russia and the Emperor and Empress of Austria.

It was also in 1887 that the Englishman Charles Wells, a confidence trickster, made his name as **'the Man who Broke the Bank at Monte-Carlo'**. In fact the Casino has always been the scene of drama — for example, **Mata Hari** shot a Russian spy there during the war.

Monaco's history is littered with romance: love between princes and princesses, most notably **Prince Rainier III and Her Serene Highness Princess Grace**, the American actress Grace Kelly, whom he married in 1956. But there were others, like Prince Antoine I who married Marie de Lorraine, one of the most beautiful and eligible aristocrats in France, in 1668. Prior to that, Louis I married a beautiful young princess of France — Catherine-Charlotte, who founded the Convent of the Visitation on Monaco, which is now the Lycée Albert 1er. All these romantic couples lived and loved in the **Prince's Palace**, high on the rock above Monte-Carlo.

Romance is such a part of life in Monaco that there used to be a special tradition for when a true marriage of opposites occurred: the local people would carry out a *ciaraviyu* — a serenade, made as discordant as possible, sung beneath the bedroom window of the newly married couple.

Prince Rainier and Grace Kelly met while she was filming *To Catch a Thief*, co-starring with Cary Grant, and Monaco has been the location of many a glamorous film. **James Bond** frequented the casino in Monte-Carlo more times, it seems, than any other fictional character. And Maximilian de Winter and his second wife met in Monte-Carlo in that great romantic novel, *Rebecca*, by Daphne du Maurier.

THE ROMANTIC PRESENT — pastimes for lovers. . .

The principality of Monaco consists of just three towns: the original town of Monaco, up on the rock; Monte-Carlo, its residential and resort centre; and the commercial centre of La Condamine.

Many world-famous events take place there, including the **Monaco Red Cross Ball**, the biggest social, artistic and charitable event in the calendar; and of course there's the **Grand Prix** every year in May.

Just being in Monaco is so romantic that it is hard to list the number of romantic pastimes. If glamour is a part of your romance, you could visit the **Casino** in all its baroque splendour. As well as the obvious gaming rooms, the recently reopened building, an extravagant folly surrounded by gardens and overlooking the sea, also has a restaurant, nightclub, bars, and a **theatre**, which was so famous that the composers **Massenet** and **Saint-Saëns** wrote operas for it, the actress **Sarah Bernhardt** appeared there, and **Diaghilev** made it the headquarters of his **Ballets-Russes de Monte-Carlo**.

Or, if nature touches a deeper chord in you, the **Jardin Exotique** is filled with over a thousand different cacti and fabulous plants from Mexico, South America and Africa, which thrive on the sun-drenched rocky outcrop, and there's also a cave you can visit which dates back to prehistoric times. And you can't possibly miss the wonderful **Oceanographical Museum**, opened in 1910, which has tucked away in its basement a huge aquarium, with seals, turtles, and a myriad brilliantly hued tropical fish.

But perhaps you prefer shopping to sightseeing. If that's the case, Monaco is not exactly the place for a bargain, but tucked behind the Hôtel de Paris is a tiny street containing nothing but shops with world-famous names. Fashion and jewellery are the things to buy here, so be prepared to spend!

And when your feet are sore and you're in need of refreshment, sit at one of the cafés or restaurants and watch the world go by. As Monaco is at the end of France and so close to Italy, most of the food and drink is predominantly French or Italian. However, there are one or two Monégasque specialities and traditions, most notably at Christmas. **Brandaminicum** is a dish made from salt cod pounded with garlic, oil and cream, surrounded by cardoons (a kind of green vegetable) in a white sauce. This is traditionally served on Christmas Eve, followed by **Barba Giuan** (Uncle John), which are stuffed fritters, and finally **fougasses**, which are flat crisp biscuits sprinkled with sweetened aniseed, rum and extract of orange flowers. All these can be found on sale in Monégasque shops at Christmas.

But, should you tire of the high life, Monaco is also an ideal centre from which to visit the many delightful towns and villages along the Côte d'Azur. **Nice, Cannes, Menton** and **Antibes** are within easy reach, there's the tiny hill-cluster village of **Eze**, and just to drive along the Moyenne Corniche is a visual treat as you round each headland and look down on yet another blue bay. Or take a trip inland into the aromatic Provençal hills to find herb-covered slopes and shady woodlands and escape from the glare of the midday sun.

DID YOU KNOW THAT. . .?

*   the miniature principality of Monaco is only 375 acres in **area**, about half the size of Central Park in New York.

* the resident **population** is 23,000, but only 2 or 3,000 of these are Monégasque citizens.

* gambling now constitutes only about 4% of **state revenue**; with there being no direct income-taxation, the main sources of the state's income are from VAT, which is very high. Banking and commerce are very important; among the main **export industries** are plastics, cosmetics and food-processing.

* the principality is within the French customs area, but issues its own **stamps**.

* the present prince, **Ranier III**, fought voluntarily in the Second World War, and received both the Croix de Guerre and the Légion d'Honneur.

* the national language of Monaco is of course French, so to say 'I love you' simply whisper '*Je t'aime*'.

LOOK OUT FOR TWO TITLES EVERY MONTH IN OUR SERIES OF EUROPEAN ROMANCES:

THE SULTAN'S FAVOURITE: Helen Brooks (Turkey)
Louisa had run to Turkey to escape the past, and run straight into Melik Haman! He swept her off her feet — but could Louisa hope to find a permanent place in his heart?

LEAP OF FAITH: Rachel Elliot (Jersey)
The notorious Marc Duval had decided that Tessa was just what he needed — but did she really need *him*? He was using her, and she knew it, but found it hard to resist him. . .

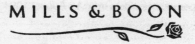

Next Month's Romances

Each month you can choose from a wide variety of romance with Mills & Boon. Below are the new titles to look out for next month, why not ask either Mills & Boon Reader Service or your Newsagent to reserve you a copy of the titles you want to buy – just tick the titles you would like and either post to Reader Service or take it to any Newsagent and ask them to order your books.

Please save me the following titles:		Please tick	✓
THE SULTAN'S FAVOURITE	Helen Brooks		
INFAMOUS BARGAIN	Daphne Clair		
A TRUSTING HEART	Helena Dawson		
MISSISSIPPI MOONLIGHT	Angela Devine		
TIGER EYES	Robyn Donald		
COVER STORY	Jane Donnelly		
LEAP OF FAITH	Rachel Elliot		
EVIDENCE OF SIN	Catherine George		
THE DAMARIS WOMAN	Grace Green		
LORD OF THE MANOR	Stephanie Howard		
INHERITANCE	Shirley Kemp		
PASSION'S PREY	Rebecca King		
DYING FOR YOU	Charlotte Lamb		
NORAH	Debbie Macomber		
PASSION BECOMES YOU	Michelle Reid		
SHADOW PLAY	Sally Wentworth		

If you would like to order these books in addition to your regular subscription from Mills & Boon Reader Service please send £1.90 per title to: Mills & Boon Reader Service, Freepost, P.O. Box 236, Croydon, Surrey, CR9 9EL, quote your Subscriber No:................................... (if applicable) and complete the name and address details below. Alternatively, these books are available from many local Newsagents including W H Smith, J Menzies, Martins and other paperback stockists from 12 August 1994.

Name:..

Address:..

....Post Code:..........................

To Retailer: If you would like to stock M&B books please contact your regular book/magazine wholesaler for details.

Full of Eastern Passion...

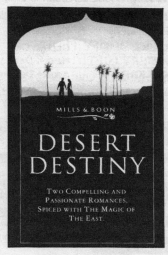

Savour the romance of the East this summer with
our two full-length compelling Romances,
wrapped together in one exciting volume.

AVAILABLE FROM 29 JULY 1994   PRICED £3.99

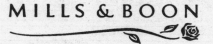

Accept 4 FREE Romances and 2 FREE gifts

FROM READER SERVICE

Here's an irresistible invitation from Mills & Boon. Please accept our offer of 4 FREE Romances, a CUDDLY TEDDY and a special MYSTERY GIFT! Then, if you choose, go on to enjoy 6 captivating Romances every month for just £1.90 each, postage and packing FREE. Plus our FREE Newsletter with author news, competitions and much more.

**Send the coupon below to:
Mills & Boon Reader Service,
FREEPOST, PO Box 236,
Croydon, Surrey CR9 9EL.**

- - - - - - - **NO STAMP REQUIRED** - - - - - - - - - - -

Yes! Please rush me 4 FREE Romances and 2 FREE gifts! Please also reserve me a Reader Service subscription. If I decide to subscribe I can look forward to receiving 6 brand new Romances for just £11.40 each month, post and packing FREE. If I decide not to subscribe I shall write to you within 10 days - I can keep the free books and gifts whatever I choose. I may cancel or suspend my subscription at any time. I am over 18 years of age.

Ms/Mrs/Miss/Mr _____ EP70R

Address _____

_____

Postcode _____ Signature _____